PRAISE FOR ROBERT J. RANDISI

D0048165

THE SIEGE BEGINS

Actually it wasn't a fight; it was more of a siege.

Once the bullets fired by the cowboys began to whistle through the *jacal,* pieces of it began falling away. The mud and roof were held up by long stakes set two inches apart. In the first barrage some of the stakes were splintered. Elfego covered his head with his arms until the firing stopped. When it was quiet he sat up and shook off the dried mud that had come down on him. The interior of the *jacal* had also filled with dust from the falling walls and ceiling.

While the cowhands were reloading, Elfego took the opportunity to take a look outside to see what was what. He saw one man moving toward the *jacal* stealthily, keeping low, gun in hand. Elfego let him get close enough to encourage him, then fired one shot that killed the man instantly. Elfego vowed not to fire a shot, and waste a bullet, unless he could be deadly accurate. Picking men off accurately, one at a time, would serve as a hell of a deterrent.

The siege began at nine o'clock. . . .

ROBERT J. RANDISI

MIRACLE
OF THE
JACAL

LEISURE BOOKS NEW YORK CITY

To Marthayn,
my very own miracle.

A LEISURE BOOK®

October 2001

Published by

Dorchester Publishing Co., Inc.
276 Fifth Avenue
New York, NY 10001

ISBN 0-8439-4923-6

Visit us on the web at www.dorchesterpub.com.

MIRACLE
OF THE
JACAL

Prologue

Socorro, New Mexico, February 1940

Elfego Baca thought it odd when, on his birthday, he was awarded a door by the people of his hometown of Socorro, New Mexico. The door had belonged to the old jailhouse, which had recently been torn down. Baca claimed to have been the very first prisoner there, in 1884, when he was nineteen years old. That was after what some people have come to call "The Miracle of the Jacal." In addition to the door, the town fathers also presented him with the key. He joked that he could have used that key all those years ago.

The night before the presentation he had been sitting in a local hotel, being interviewed by a

9

writer for *The Albuquerque Tribune,* which would later publish the interview as part of a birthday tribute to the man who was—without argument—the most famous Mexican lawman of all time.

However, at the time of the interview Elfego was seventy-five years old and had recently been defeated in an attempt to win an election as a district judge. He was a lawyer and had been for many years, but since 1924 he had been unsuccessfully seeking some sort of elected office.

As he sat with the reporter on the eve of his birthday he had talked about all his various business ventures over the years, including once owning a restaurant that had not stayed open very long. . . .

Elfego shifted his weight in the hardwood chair as he stared across the table at the young reporter from *The Albuquerque Tribune.* At seventy-five he had become what some people might describe as "portly," and sitting for too long often made his butt go numb. It didn't help that he continued to wear a gun on his hip—at this time of his life, a .32-caliber revolver—for which he had to make allowances every time he sat. He felt it necessary to wear the gun this way, however, since he still had many old enemies who would like to see him dead, and wearing the gun in a concealed fashion was illegal.

The reporter had been waiting for him when

he entered the hotel dining room. Elfego had had second thoughts about agreeing to the interview, but since it was to be a birthday tribute he agreed, even though most of these interviews eventually centered around one particular incident in his life. He'd had such a long and varied existence, he often wondered why that was. Why was there only one thing people were always interested in hearing about?

Well, maybe this time would be different. . . .

"What was the restaurant called?" the reporter asked.

"Elfego's Café," Elfego replied, thinking back. "That was in 1930, I believe, when I was living in Socorro on Sixth and Gold. I owned the building then and opened the café on the ground floor. It was not a very successful venture, I am afraid."

"No?"

"I do not know why, exactly," Elfego said. "The food was actually quite good. I hired a cook from—"

"Well," the reporter said, interrupting him as gently as possible, "to tell you the truth, Senor Baca, I am not so much interested in your life as a café owner."

"Well, I have had many lives," Elfego said. "I have had many careers. A sheriff, a lawyer—ah, I was a district attorney, at one time . . . also, I was once mayor of—"

"Excuse me, senor," the reporter said, interrupting yet again, "but . . . it is your life as a lawman that I am most interested in talking to you about."

Elfego closed his mouth and stared at the young man from beneath heavy lids. He knew what the man wanted to hear. How many times could he tell the same story? Why did something that had happened fifty-six years before still hold such fascination for people? Apparently, this interview was to be no different from any of the others.

Unless . . .

"Senor?" The reporter was afraid that the old lawman had fallen asleep.

"Yes?"

"As I said—"

"It is not my *life* as a lawman you want to hear about, is it?" Elfego asked impatiently.

"Well—"

"It is the story of one incident, is it not?"

"Well, yes, but—"

"You have heard the story before?"

"Yes, but not from you—"

"How many times . . ." Baca said, shaking his head.

Looking uncomfortable, the reporter said, "If you do not wish to discuss it—"

"No," Elfego said, cutting him off, "I *will* tell you the story . . ."

"Excellent! How did—"

". . . but I will also do something that I have never done before."

"And . . . what is that?" the reporter asked carefully.

Elfego leaned forward, reached back to massage life back into his left buttock, and said, "I will tell you the story the way it actually happened."

"You mean . . ."

"*Sí,*" Elfego Baca said, sitting back in his chair again, a crafty smile on his face, "I will tell you the true story of 'The Miracle of the Jacal.'"

One
The Miracle of the Jacal

Chapter One

When nineteen-year-old Elfego Baca arrived at Milligan's Plaza that fall he had no idea that, in the span of three days, he would make his reputation—a reputation that would stay with him for the rest of his life.

But that's getting ahead of the story. . . .

Elfego Baca had been working in Socorro, east of the Friscos, for a storekeeper named Jose Baca— probably a distant relation—for $20 a month, plus room and board. Several days earlier Jose Baca's brother-in-law, Pedro Saraccino, came into the store. He was the deputy sheriff in Lower Frisco.

There were three small Mexican villages along that stretch of the San Francisco River near the Arizona border. The three villages were known collectively as San Francisco, or Frisco. Individually they were called the Lower, Middle, and Upper Plazas, or the Frisco Plazas. And finally, the Upper Plaza was also called Milligan's Plaza.

Originally settled by Mexicans during the 1870s, the area saw an influx, in the 1880s, of Texas cattlemen who had established ranches in the surrounding valleys. Milligan's Saloon became the gathering place for the cowhands from these spreads, letting them blow off some steam when they weren't working.

Deputy Saraccino was upset when he entered the store. Since the two men spoke frequently, Elfego Baca could see this and asked what the trouble was.

"The cowboys are getting out of hand, Elfego," Saraccino complained.

"Then why don't you do something about it, Pedro?" Elfego asked. "Make some arrests."

Saraccino looked down and away. "If I was to try to make any arrests, I am sure they would kill me."

"Well, what are they doing that is so terrible?"

Jose Baca came over at that point, also wanting to hear the story of what was going on in the Friscos.

"They humiliate our people," Saraccino said. "They never pick on *gringos,* but our people . . ."

Wide-eyed, Jose Baca asked, "What do they do, Pedro?"

Saraccino looked around to be sure they were alone, then moved closer to the two men.

"I will tell you of something that happened just before I left," the deputy said.

Both Bacas leaned forward and listened with interest.

"They are from the Slaughter spread, these men," Saraccino said. "Because John Slaughter is the biggest rancher in the valley, his men feel they can do anything they want. Do you know 'El Burro'?"

"I have heard of him," Jose said.

"He has a cantina in the Friscos, does he not?" Elfego asked.

"*Sí,*" the deputy said, "and in his own place they take him, spread him out on the bar top and . . . humiliate him in a way no man should be humiliated."

"*Madre de dios,*" Jose said, crossing himself.

"Embarrassing and humiliating, yes, but—" Elfego started, but the lawman cut him off.

"That is not all," he said. "A customer named Epitacio Martinez took offense at this treatment of El Burro and protested loudly."

"And what did they do?" Jose asked.

"They grabbed him when they were finished with poor El Burro. They tied his hands and feet, then marked off thirty paces from him and . . . used him as a human target. They bet drinks on who was the better shot. They shot him four times."

"Did he die?" Jose asked.

"Miracle of miracles, no," Saraccino said, "but . . ." He shook his head.

With little sympathy for his friend, Elfego Baca stood up straight and said, "You should be ashamed."

"Elfego!" Jose Baca said.

Elfego ignored his employer.

"You are the law, Pedro," he said to the deputy. "You should not allow these men to do these terrible things to our people."

"I know," Saraccino said, "and I am ashamed . . . but I am also alive, Elfego."

Elfego Baca shook his head. At his age he knew no fear, and he was incensed by this treatment of his people by the *gringo* cowboys who worked for John Slaughter.

"If you like," Saraccino said rashly, "you can take my badge and do my job for me."

"I will do it!" Elfego replied.

"Elfego," Jose Baca said, "you are foolhardy."

"They are many, Elfego," Saraccino said. "If you arrest even one, you will have to deal with them all."

"Then I will," the young Mexican said. "You take me back to the Friscos with you, Saraccino. I will not take your job, but I will appoint myself a lawman, and as a self-appointed deputy I will make the arrest. We will put a stop to this horrible treatment now."

Saraccino did not know whether to admire the young man's courage . . . or pity him.

Chapter Two

It was decided that Elfego and the deputy, Saraccino, would leave the next day. They agreed to meet the next morning in front of the livery.

Elfego did not own a horse so he went into the livery to rent one.

"I do not have a horse to rent you, Elfego," the liveryman said. "But I do have a mule and a buckboard."

Elfego would not be caught dead riding a mule into the Friscos, so he rented both the mule and the buckboard after borrowing some money from Jose Baca. Elfego then went back to Jose Baca's store to pack his meager belongings for the trip.

He had been given a room by Jose over the store, and now the elder Baca watched as the younger packed.

"Will you be coming back, Elfego?"

"I do not know, Jose," Elfego said, pausing to stand straight and look at his employer. "I think perhaps I was born to be a lawman, like my father."

"That profession did not turn out very well for your father," Jose reminded him.

This was true. Francisco Baca had been marshal of a town called Belen, forty-five miles north of Socorro. During that time he shot and killed two cowboys, after which he himself was arrested. It was only because Elfego and some of his friends broke his father out of jail that Francisco did not die at the end of a rope.

"I will do better," Elfego said, "and I will begin in the Friscos."

"I still do not think this wise, Elfego," Jose said. "If you decide that you want to come back, though, you will still have a job here waiting for you."

"Thank you, Jose," Elfego said, "but even before Saraccino came to town with this story I had decided that I am not cut out for the life of a storekeeper—honorable profession that it is," he hurriedly added.

"I can do nothing but wish you luck, then."

"And have supper with me tonight," Elfego said. "A farewell supper."

"Done," Jose Baca said, and went back downstairs to tend his store.

Elfego walked to the window and looked out.

At a young age he had already had many adventures, like rescuing his father from jail and befriending and riding with Billy the Kid. Now, however, it was time for him to find his life's work.

Perhaps it was the law.

Only time would tell.

Rather than having supper out somewhere, the store owner insisted that Elfego have it with him and his wife at their house at the south end of town.

Angelina Baca looked on Elfego as the son she never had, and having the same last name did nothing to hurt the illusion. Over supper she argued with him as a mother would.

"You will get hurt," she said, "or worse, you will get killed."

"I understand the dangers, Angelina," Elfego said, "but I am quite good with my guns."

"That is true," Jose Baca said, "and he has the heart of a lion."

Angelina Baca gave her husband a dirty look that forced him silent.

"The heart of a lion," she said with contempt, "simply means it is a bigger target for a bullet."

"Well," Jose said, somewhat reluctantly, "she has a point. . . ."

The look Elfego gave him was not a dirty one, but it silenced him nevertheless.

"This is something a man has to do, Angelina," he said.

"A man!" she replied. "You are still a boy."

Elfego knew where her protests were coming from, and he felt great affection for her because of it.

"I am nineteen, Angelina," he said calmly. "No longer a boy."

"A gun does not make you a man," she said, trying a new argument.

"It has nothing to do with a gun," he responded. "It has to do with a sense of justice."

"There is already law in the Friscos to take care of justice."

"That's where you are wrong," Elfego said. "The law there cannot handle it, and that is why I must go."

"But—"

"And I must call a halt to all argument about it," he said, holding up his hand. "Please, I would like to enjoy the company of both of you my last night in Socorro."

"But . . . you will be coming back to Socorro, no?" she asked.

"I am sure I will," he said, "again and again. This is my home. But first I must do what I must do."

"But Elfego—"

"You heard him, Angelina," Jose Baca said, speaking with more force than he had in some time. "The decision is Elfego's, and he does not wish to discuss it any further."

Angelina Baca closed her mouth and looked at both men in turn. Had she shed a tear they might have allowed the argument to go on a little longer. But she knew that in the end she would still lose. Come morning Elfego would be leaving Socorro, and she did not want his last thoughts of her to be ones filled with anger.

"Very well," she said. "This is as it must be. I will fetch the coffee."

She cleared the table of supper plates and went into the kitchen.

"I have something for you," Jose said after she had left.

"What is it?"

The older man rose and walked to a chest of drawers. He opened the bottom one and brought out something that was wrapped in cloth. He unwrapped it, dropped the cloth into the drawer, and returned to the table. Upon it he laid a gun and holster.

"Your gun," Elfego said.

"I have not worn it in many years."

Despite this, it was not a very old weapon. Elfego drew it forth from the holster. It was a Colt, with blued metal and barely worn grips.

"It is a wonderful weapon," Elfego said, "but I have a gun, Jose."

"I know that," Jose Baca said, "but somehow I think you might need another, eh?"

Considering how many cowboys Saraccino said he would have to go up against once they reached the Friscos, Elfego was suddenly sure that Jose was right.

He slid the gun back into the holster. "*Gracias,* Jose."

"Let us put it aside before she comes back with the coffee," Jose said. "I will leave it by the door for you . . . and you will not forget to take it, eh? Perhaps this way I can be with you, if only in spirit."

"You will be with me always, Jose," Elfego said. He put his hand on the gun just before Jose removed it. "And I am very grateful for and honored by this gift."

"Use it well," Jose said, "that is all I ask. Use it well, be smart, and stay alive."

Elfego smiled. "Three very good pieces of advice I intend to take to heart, my friend."

Chapter Three

Though not very long, the ride from Socorro to the Friscos was not an easy one. On horseback it would have been no problem, but with the mule pulling a buckboard it became a trial. In fact, there were times when Elfego and Saraccino almost had to push the mule up a hill.

In the end they arrived late and rode directly to Saraccino's house in Lower Frisco, rather than go to Milligan's Plaza in Upper Frisco, where most of the trouble had taken place.

Saraccino's wife, Carmen, greeted Elfego warmly, having met him once or twice in Socorro when she was visiting her brother, Jose Baca. She had prepared a late supper for them, which she served, then left them to talk, promising to return to bring them coffee and pie.

"Tomorrow," Elfego said, when she had gone, "I will go to El Burro's saloon in Milligan's Plaza and talk to him."

"If you go in the afternoon you may be able to avoid Slaughter's men."

"Pedro," Elfego said, "have you forgotten it is not my goal to avoid these men? I am here to arrest them."

"Perhaps El Burro will not want to identify them."

"There were witnesses, were there not?"

"*Sí,*" Saraccino said, "many, but it will be very hard to locate them now."

"Then I will simply have to wait," Elfego said. "If everything you have said about these men is true, they will break the law again, and I will be there to arrest them."

"Elfego," Saraccino said, "you will need help. . . ."

"I have you."

Saraccino looked away, ashamed.

"Very well, then," Elfego said, "I will do it myself."

"Perhaps," the deputy said, "there is a better way."

"What would you suggest?"

"We could ride out and talk to John Slaughter about his men," Saraccino said. "Perhaps if we warned him—"

"This you would do with me?" Elfego asked, interrupting him. "You would not be afraid?"

"I would be afraid," Saraccino said, "but *sí,* I would ride there with you."

Elfego thought a moment. "The goal is to stop this mistreatment of our people. Perhaps John Slaughter could do this by speaking with his men about it, and perhaps not. *Muy bien,* we will go and speak to him tomorrow."

"Tomorrow?" Saraccino asked. "So soon?"

"The sooner the better, Pedro," Elfego said, "before someone else is humiliated, or hurt. And what of Epitacio Martinez?"

"What about him?"

"We must find out if he died as a result of his wounds. If he did, then the men who shot him are murderers. They will have to be arrested, no matter what John Slaughter says."

"I will find out first thing in the morning," Saraccino said.

"Bien," Elfego said. He dipped the last tortilla into Carmen Saraccino's wonderful sauce. "Your wife is a wondrous cook."

"Sí," Saraccino said, "and a wonderful woman. It would be a shame to see her widowed at such a young age."

Elfego looked across the table at Saraccino and said, "I see your point, Pedro."

"Do you?"

"Yes," Elfego said, "and I do not hold it against you that you do not want to die and leave your wife widowed, but . . ."

"Sí?"

"Do not take offense," Elfego said, "but if you are were worried about that, perhaps you are in the wrong job."

"Perhaps you are right," Saraccino said, "but at the moment it is the only job I can get."

Elfego nodded and pushed away his empty plate. At that moment Carmen entered, smiling shyly. It was then Elfego realized she had been listening at the door, and that Pedro Saraccino had been speaking as much for her benefit as for his own.

"Ready for pie?" she asked.

"*Sí,*" Elfego said, "we are ready."

Later that night, Carmen Saraccino found Elfego sitting on the front porch, smoking a cigar and cleaning his two guns.

"Where is Pedro?" he asked.

"Asleep."

"And why are you not asleep?"

"I wanted to talk to you."

Carmen Saraccino was several years younger than her husband, but seven or eight years older than Elfego. She was a lovely woman, with masses of black hair that cascaded down her back in shimmering waves, and a figure like an hourglass.

"About what?"

"Pedro," she said. "Elfego, I know he talked to you about me."

"Yes."

"I do not want to see either one of you be killed."

"I do not want that either."

"Then why do this?" she asked. "Why go against these Slaughter men? These *gringos*?"

"Because justice must be done, Carmen."

"I do not want to be a widow," she said.

"I know," Elfego answered. "No one wants that."

"I did not want Pedro to take the job as deputy," she explained. "I made him promise not to do anything foolish. I made him promise, Elfego, not to get killed."

"I understand that, Carmen."

"Do you?" she asked. "Do you really?"

"Yes."

"Then don't shame him into helping you," she pleaded. "Don't shame him into getting himself killed."

"I will not shame him," Elfego said, "or try to force him to do anything."

"By doing his job for him you shame him."

"Carmen," he said, "this is something I must do. This is about me, not about Pedro. I will not think less of him if he does not stand with me against the *gringos*."

She hugged herself, though it was not cold, and said, "Perhaps you will not think less of him . . ."

She left the sentence unfinished and went back inside.

Chapter Four

John B. Slaughter had been the first American to arrive in the valley and stake a claim for himself. He had brought many men with him, driving many more horses, and established what had become the largest spread in the area. As such the ranch employed many men, most of whom he could not possibly get to know personally. That he had to leave to his foreman, Jack Perham.

Perham came to Slaughter, who was sitting in his office at his desk, going over his accounts.

"Sir?"

"Yes, Jack?"

"Two men to see you, boss."

"Who are they?"

"They say they're lawmen."

Slaughter looked up at his foreman.

"Any proof?"

"One of them's wearing a deputy sheriff's badge."

"You know him?"

"No," Perham said, "but I don't go into the Friscos much."

"No," Slaughter said, "neither do I."

Slaughter did his banking and his business in Socorro.

"All right," he said, closing his account books, "show them in here, Jack."

"Yes, sir."

Slaughter stood, straightened his vest and shirt. He was not a tall man, but neither was he ever shown disrespect. The name Slaughter was known throughout the Southwest. Whatever these lawmen wanted he was sure they'd treat him with respect, and he would return the favor—until they gave him reason to do otherwise.

By the time Elfego Baca was dressed and ready to go the next morning, Saraccino had already been out, checking on the condition of Epitacio Martinez. The men found breakfast on the table when they entered the kitchen.

"Martinez did not die," Saraccino told Elfego over *heuvos rancheros*.

"Good," Elfego said, "then he can testify."

"No," the lawman said. "He left town."

"Where did he go?"

"I don't know," Saraccino said, "but I heard

that when he left he was moving as fast as he could, considering his wounds."

"Foolish," Elfego said. "He could be dead on the trail, for all we know."

"Either way," Saraccino said, "he's no help to us."

They finished their breakfast and went outside. The lawman had been busy. He'd saddled his horse, and one for Elfego as well, a good-looking five-year-old horse as white as snow.

"Where did you find him?" Elfego asked.

"At the livery," the deputy said. "Left behind as payment. I rented him for you."

"With the saddle?"

"With the saddle."

Elfego patted the animal's powerful neck, touched the leather of the black saddle, and said, "You did well."

After that they mounted up and rode out to the Slaughter ranch, where they presented themselves to the foreman, Jack Perham.

Jack Perham came out of the house and said to Elfego and Saraccino, "Come with me. The boss can spare you a few minutes."

"*Gracias,*" Elfego said.

Perham let them into the house, wondering why it was the youth without the badge who did the talking.

He showed them down the hall to John Slaughter's office, where his boss waited to entertain his visitors.

"Deputy," Slaughter said as the two men entered. "That'll be all, Jack."

"I could stay, boss."

"I'll call you if I need you."

"Yes, sir."

Perham withdrew, and Slaughter took a look at his guests. The man with the badge was in his thirties, not tall, his clothes well worn. The other was a youth, barely twenty by the look of him, but tall and well built and, from the look in his eyes and despite the fact that the other man wore the badge of authority, the more confident.

"I'm John Slaughter," he said. "And you are?"

"Uh, Deputy Sheriff Pedro Saraccino, Mr. Slaughter."

"Elfego Baca is my name," the younger one said.

"Baca?" Slaughter said. "I know that name."

"It is fairly common."

Not only was the storekeeper's name Jose Baca, but the two brothers of Elfego's father arrested for killing had also been named Baca—no relation.

A common name, indeed.

"What can I do for you gents, then?" Slaughter asked. He walked around behind his desk and sat down. "Please, have a seat and tell me."

Chapter Five

When Saraccino looked to Elfego for guidance, it did not go unnoticed by Slaughter. The young man was in charge here—or so he thought.

Elfego and Saraccino sat, and Slaughter waited patiently.

"Senor Slaughter," Elfego said, "we come here seeking your help."

"My help."

"Well, perhaps 'cooperation' would be a better word."

"What kind of cooperation?"

"We ask that you keep your men from humiliating the people of the Friscos—specifically, the Upper Friscos."

"As far as I know, my men take their . . . leisure in Milligan's Plaza."

"Yes," Elfego said, "at Milligan's Saloon, and some other places."

"Well, what sort of humiliation are we talking about?" Slaughter asked. "I mean, I know cowhands can get rowdy at times, and a little playful—"

"This goes beyond playful, I am afraid," Elfego said. "They stripped one man and ... altered him, then used another man for target practice when he protested."

"My men did this?" Slaughter asked.

"Six or seven of them."

"Do you have any names?"

"No."

"Any witnesses to describe them?"

"No."

"Then why should I believe that these were my men you're talking about?"

Elfego looked directly into Slaughter's eyes. Both men saw the same thing—stubbornness, confidence, and just a little arrogance. It was no surprise to Elfego Baca to see this in a forty-three-year-old rancher with a reputation, but John Horton Slaughter was surprised to see it in one so young.

"Because I am telling you."

"I see a badge on this man's chest," Slaughter said, "though he doesn't act like any lawman I ever knew. What business is any of this to you, Mr. Baca?"

"I am a self-appointed deputy, Mr. Slaughter," Elfego said.

Slaughter found that amusing.

"Self-appointed?" He shook his head. "What sort of authority do you believe that gives you?"

"The authority to arrest and transport to Socorro any man who breaks the law."

Slaughter leaned back in his chair.

"Mr. Baca," he said, "I'm gonna tell you this. You do what you think you've got to do."

"Then you will not warn your men to stay away from Milligan's Plaza?"

"No," Slaughter said, "I won't. My men need a place to blow off steam."

"Will you tell them to find another way to . . . blow off steam, as you say?"

Slaughter spread his hands.

"You haven't shown me any proof that they need to find a new way."

Elfego stood up abruptly, Saraccino a beat behind him.

"When I arrest one of them and take him in," Elfego said, "perhaps that will be proof enough."

"Perhaps," Slaughter said. "But I have to warn you, the rest of my men are not just going to stand around and watch some self-appointed lawman arrest one of their own."

Elfego shrugged and said, "What will be, will be."

"Well," Slaughter said, "it will be interesting, at least. Good day."

Elfego turned and left without returning the wish, Saraccino close on his heels.

Chapter Six

"That did not accomplish much," Saraccino said to Elfego as they rode back to Lower Frisco.

"Perhaps it did," Elfego said.

"Like what?"

"We know where Slaughter stands."

"I do not know where he stands."

"We cannot expect any assistance from him," Elfego explained, "unless we can prove to him beyond the shadow of a doubt that his men are mistreating the people of the Friscos."

"And how will we—how will you do that?" Saraccino asked carefully.

"I will spend time in Upper Frisco," Elfego said. "I will stay there, and I will wait, and when the time comes, I will act."

Saraccino admitted Elfego Baca's youthful courage, but feared for his young friend's life.

After Elfego and Saraccino left, Slaughter went looking for Jack Perham. He found him out by the stable, looking over some horses.

"Jack."

Perham turned at the sound of his name.

"What's up, boss? Those two leave already?'

"They're gone," Slaughter said.

"What'd they want?"

"Something about our men behaving badly in the Friscos, at Milligan's Plaza. What's been going on?"

"Well," Perham said, "I know the men go into Milligan's to blow off some steam."

"That's what I said," Slaughter replied, "but they said there was more than that going on."

"If there is, I don't know about it, boss."

"Well, find out," Slaughter said. "I don't want any of our men doing anything that's gonna get them arrested, understand?"

"Yes, sir," Perham said. "Who was that young fella, boss?"

"Said his name's Elfego Baca."

"Never heard of him."

"His father was a marshal for a while," Slaughter said. He'd remembered Francisco Baca's name after the two men had left.

"He don't look like he's old enough to be a lawman."

"Maybe not," Slaughter said, "but he's appointed himself one."

Perham laughed and asked, "What kind of authority does that give him?"

"I guess he intends to show us," Slaughter said.

"The men will run right over him."

"I don't want them running right over him," Slaughter said, flaring up, "I want them to stay away from him. Make that clear."

"Yes, sir," Perham said. "Do you want me to stop the men from goin' to Milligan's?"

"No," Slaughter said. He leaned on the corral and began to look over the horses in it. "No, they do need a place to let loose, and I don't want them all to have to pay because a few of them are getting out of hand. Who do you trust, Jack?"

"How do you mean?"

"I mean, which of the men do you rely on the most?"

"Well . . . Dave Matthews and Rob Thomas can be trusted to do their jobs."

"And keep their heads?"

"Usually."

"Good," Slaughter said. "I want you to go to Milligan's with the men from time to time, and when you can't, have Matthews or Thomas keep an eye out."

"Yes, sir."

"This Elfego Baca might just be looking to arrest someone to make himself look good, or to make some kind of a name for himself," Slaughter said. "If he's the troublemaker, he's gonna have to pay for it."

"You want me to tell the men that, too?"

Slaughter thought a moment. "No, let them go with their instincts in that one. Good-looking animals, Jack. These for the Army?"

"Yes, sir. We'll be showin' them off tomorrow."

"Good," Slaughter said. "I'm going back inside to finish up the accounts."

"I'll take care of everything, boss. You can count on me."

"I know I can, Jack," Slaughter said. "Thanks."

Later, Perham met with Dave Matthews and Rob Thomas and a few of the other men.

"This has to be about what happened the other day with those two Mexes," Thomas said.

"The boys went too far, shootin' pieces off that one fella," Perham said.

"Well," Matthews said, "the law didn't do nothin', so why worry?"

"Nobody pressed charges," Perham said, "and the deputy wouldn't move on his own. This fella Baca, he might be different."

"From what you said, he ain't near old enough to be a problem," Thomas said.

"He's wearin' a gun," Perham said, "he can be a problem."

"What do you want us to do, boss?" Matthews asked.

"If he makes a move against any of us," the foreman said, "he's gonna have to pay."

"He ain't the law?" Thomas asked,

"Self-appointed deputy," Perham said.

"Well, that don't give him hardly no authority at all," Dave Matthews said.

"None," Perham said. "I want you boys to remember that."

"What about the deputy?" Thomas asked.

"He ain't gonna do a thing," Perham said. "He ain't got it in him. You can see that lookin' into his eyes."

"And the kid?" Thomas asked.

"He's got weird eyes," Perham said, "old eyes. He'd go to the wall, I'm sure of it."

"It ain't gonna be easy gettin' the boys to lay off," Matthews said.

"We don't have to," Perham said. "Just watch for this young fella, and back each other up. We ain't about to let no self-appointed deputy run roughshod over the Slaughter spread. Understand?"

The other men nodded, and Thomas said, "We understand, boss."

"After all," Perham added, "he's just a damned Mexican."

Chapter Seven

Elfego went to the Upper Plaza the next day, but nothing happened then or the day after. He spent each night with Pedro and Carmen Saraccino, telling them over dinner how quiet it had been in Milligan's Plaza.

"That is good," Carmen said. "Maybe the word has gone out about you, Elfego?"

"I doubt that, Carmen," Elfego said. "There is no word to go out about me that would frighten away John Slaughter's cowboys."

"What about your riding with Billy the Kid?" she asked. "Maybe they heard about that?"

"Not unless you or Pedro told them," Elfego said. "No one else in the Friscos knows about that."

"What about you breaking your father out of

jail?" she asked, desperately looking for something that would convince Elfego that his job was done so he would leave the Friscos.

"It has only been two days, Carmen," Elfego said. "I am going to give it a lot more time before I give up."

Carmen gave her husband a look that said, "You say something!" but there was nothing for the deputy to say.

While Carmen cleared the dinner dishes, Elfego and Saraccino went outside on the front porch and lit up cigars.

"Perhaps I should find a hotel room, Pedro," Elfego said. "I think your wife would like me to leave."

"Do not take offense, Elfego," Saraccino said. "It is not that she wants you to leave our home. She would like you to leave the Friscos and go back to Socorro."

"Ah . . . I see."

"She would be very embarrassed if you left our home and went to a hotel," Saraccino said. "She would also think that you did not think her a good hostess."

"Then I will not leave," the younger man said. "It is difficult, though, to eat dinner sitting across from those eyes every night, eh?"

Saraccino knew what he meant. Elfego was not complimenting his wife on her beautiful eyes. He was speaking of eyes that could look into a man's soul and make him feel tremendous guilt. As her husband, he had fallen prey to those eyes many times.

"Perhaps tomorrow there will be trouble," Elfego said. "I can make my arrest and go back to Socorro with my prisoner."

"And perhaps John Slaughter did talk to his men after we left his ranch," Saraccino offered. "Perhaps there will be no more trouble from the Slaughter cowboys."

"That is the way we would all like it to happen, Pedro," Elfego said. "But John Slaughter did not strike me as the kind of man who would scare easily—certainly not because of a self-appointed deputy. I think I will have to prove myself to him and his men before I gain their respect."

"Elfego," Saraccino said, "I know how good you are with a gun, and when you go to Milligan's Plaza you are wearing two, which makes you twice as dangerous."

"Stop flattering me and get to the point, Pedro."

"I am not flattering you," Saraccino said, "I am stating fact. You are very good with the *pistolas,* as fine a *pistolero* as I have ever seen, but the Slaughter cowboys, they are many. A hundred, perhaps more."

"Certainly not all in town at the same time?"

"A good many of them."

"I appreciate what you're saying, Pedro," Elfego said. "Even with two guns I am no match for a hundred cowboys."

"*Sí*, that is my point."

"And a point well taken, I assure you."

"But you will still go to Milligan's Plaza?"

Elfego nodded. "Day in and day out, until something happens."

"That is what I was afraid you would say."

Chapter Eight

The next day Elfego met a man named Lopez, who happened to be the justice of the peace in Upper Frisco. In fact, the man approached him on the street and introduced himself. He was in his fifties, wearing a three-piece suit, the vest of which was stretched over a prodigious belly. His manner was officious, to say the least.

"I have been hearing things about you," the man continued after the introduction.

"What things, senor?"

"Apparently you have appointed yourself as a deputy?" Lopez asked.

"That is true."

"This concerns me," the man said. "By what authority?"

"My own."

"And what do you intend to do with this . . . authority?" the J.P. asked.

At that moment several cowboys came riding down the main street, firing their guns. For the most part they were shooting into the air, but the cracking sound of glass breaking made it clear that not all of their shots went straight into the sky.

A few people had to scatter in the streets to avoid being trampled; others simply dove for cover, not knowing where the shots were being aimed.

The cowboys rode right up to Milligan's Saloon, which was across the street from where Elfego and Lopez were standing. They fired several more rounds, some of which struck the facade of the building, then dismounted and went inside.

"I want to stop things like that from happening," Elfego said. "Such things should not be allowed."

"They cannot be stopped," Lopez said.

"Why not?"

"They are John Slaughter's men."

"And as such they are above the law?" Elfego asked.

"Mr. Baca," Lopez said, "John Slaughter has one hundred and fifty men in his employ. If they wanted to they could level the Lower, Middle, and Upper Friscos. When they come into town they fire their weapons harmlessly—"

"Harmlessly?" Elfego asked. "I heard glass

51

breaking, sir. Have they ever killed anyone?"

"A few dogs, perhaps, some chickens—"

"And the people in the street who were almost ridden down?"

"Precautions must always be taken when crossing the street."

"Is the Slaughter outfit so important to you that they can get away with anything?"

"To me?" Lopez asked. "Not to me personally, Mr. Baca." Elfego noticed how the man studiously avoided calling him "deputy." That was fair. After all, he was not wearing a badge of the office. "They are important to the town, to the merchants here," Lopez said. "And not only to the Friscos, but to Socorro, as well."

"I do not believe they would be allowed to indiscriminately shoot up Socorro, sir," Elfego said. "Not the town itself, or its people."

"This is not Socorro, sir," the J.P. responded. "If you do anything to drive the Slaughter outfit's business away from us, you would be doing a service to no one."

"If I can keep them from shooting pieces off of anyone, or from humiliating anyone," Elfego said, "or, God forbid, killing anyone, I do a service to us all, I think."

"You are young," Lopez said. "You obviously do not understand give-and-take."

"I understand it very well," Elfego said. "I simply do not believe the people of the Friscos need to give so much."

At that moment a young man came walking up to them, and both turned to see what he wanted. He was from the town, only a couple of years older than Elfego, though not so self-assured.

"Deputy Baca?" he asked.

"That's that." Elfego took this opportunity to dismiss the justice of the peace. "If you will excuse me, sir?"

Lopez looked at Elfego, then at the other man. He shook his head and walked away.

"What can I do for you, senor?" Elfego asked the man.

"It is, perhaps, what I can do for you," the man said. "My name is Francisquito Naranjo. I live here in Upper San Francisco and am acquainted with the deputy, Pedro Saraccino."

"Yes?"

"Pedro told me what you are doing," Naranjo said, "and I would like to offer my assistance."

"Franciscquito—"

"Just Francisco, *por favor.*"

"Bien," Elfego said. "Francisco, did Pedro tell you that my authority is my own?"

"Sí, I am aware of that."

"And you wish to help in spite of that?"

"Sí," Naranjo said. "No one else will do what must be done. If you will have me, I am with you."

"You are a brave man," Elfego said. He looked at the worn gun Naranjo was wearing tucked

53

into his belt. He, himself, had the gun Jose Baca had given him strapped around his waist, and his own weapon tucked into his belt. He couldn't fault the man for not being able to afford a gunbelt.

"Can you use that?" Elfego asked, indicating the gun with his chin.

"I can hit what I aim at," Naranjo said, "usually."

"This will be dangerous."

"I know."

"All right, then," Elfego said. "In my unofficial capacity as deputy, I hereby unofficially deputize you."

Naranjo smiled broadly and said, "*Gracias,* Deputy Baca."

"Call me Elfego."

"What do we do first, Elfego?"

"Well . . . I've been waiting for some trouble so I can make my move—"

At that moment two cowboys came out of Milligan's, and one struck the other a blow on the head with his pistol. Elfego recognized the cowboy with the gun as one of the men who had come riding into town firing weapons into the air. If he hadn't reloaded he probably had one shot left in the gun.

The cowboy with the gun struck the other man two more times. "And maybe this is it," Elfego said to Naranjo. "Come on."

Chapter Nine

Elfego and Naranjo approached the two men. They could see others watching from the windows of Milligan's Saloon, as well as from behind the saloon's batwing doors.

"Stand off to my right," Elfego said to Naranjo as they walked. "Not behind me."

"*Sí.*"

"Don't draw your gun unless I do."

Naranjo nodded.

The assailant raised his gun to strike the other man again. The victim staggered, blood flowing from a gash in his forehead.

"Stop right there!" Elfego shouted. "I am a self-appointed deputy, and I say—"

Instead of stopping, the man turned quickly and fired a shot. The bullet took Elfego's hat from his head. The men in the saloon laughed out loud, but stopped laughing when the man pulled the trigger again and the hammer fell on an empty chamber.

Elfego drew his weapon, as did Naranjo.

"You are under arrest," he said to the man.

"Who says?"

"I do."

"Who are you?"

"Elfego Baca, self-appointed deputy."

"You can't arrest me."

Elfego took one step and plucked the man's empty gun from his hand. The man who had received the clubbing had fallen to the ground in a seated position and was holding his head in his hands.

"I can," Elfego said, "and I am."

He kept a wary eye on the men who were watching from inside Milligan's.

"Let's go."

The man looked toward the saloon and shouted, "You gonna let him take me?"

"If they try to interfere," Elfego said, "I'll shoot you. It is your choice."

Some of the men came out through the batwing doors, their hands floating above their guns.

"Hold it!" the assailant said. "He means it. He'll put a bullet in me."

"Don't worry, Marcus," one of the men said. "He won't be able to keep you. We'll talk to the boss."

Elfego thought that by "boss" the man meant John Slaughter.

"Do you know who I work for?" his prisoner asked.

"I think I do."

"And you're still gonna lock me up?"

"*Sí.*"

"Where are you gonna take him?" someone called out. "There's no jail up here."

Elfego looked around and saw the justice of the peace standing across the street.

"What's your name?" he asked his prisoner.

"McCarty."

"Come with me."

They walked away from the saloon and approached the J.P.

"What are you doing?" Lopez asked.

"I have arrested this man," Elfego said. "Will you try him here?"

"I will not hear a case against this man," Lopez said. "I told you, I warned you, it would not bode well for you to make an arrest. You are on your own."

"Not quite," Elfego said with a nod toward Naranjo.

"He won't do you any good against all of them." The justice of the peace jerked his head in the direction of the saloon. Elfego looked over and saw that about thirty cowboys had come out onto the boardwalk.

"Elfego?" Naranjo said.

Elfego wondered if his unofficial deputy was having second thoughts.

"Take it easy, Francisco," he said. "They won't try anything. They have no leader."

"Yet," Lopez said.

Elfego looked at the J.P.

"You tell anybody who asks that I took McCarty to the jail in Lower Frisco. Tell them that the deputy there has nothing to do with this. And tell them I will be taking him to the county seat in the morning. Can you remember all that?"

"I will remember," Lopez said. "You remember that I warned you . . . Deputy."

"I will remember . . . Your Honor." He looked at Naranjo. "Keep your gun on him."

"*Sí*, Elfego."

"If his friends try anything, follow my lead," he said, "but he will get the first bullet. *Comprende?*"

"*Comprendo.*"

"Yeah, *comprende* this, you dirty Mex," McCarty said. "You'll never hold me."

"We will see, McCarty," Elfego said, prodding the man with his gun. "We will see."

Chapter Ten

The word went out of McCarty's arrest and the cowboys were up in arms, furious that a Mexican—and a self-appointed lawman at that—had arrested one of theirs. The incensed cowboys were not all from John Slaughter's spread, but from a few of the others, as well. A man named A. C. Wilson, who had a spread even closer to Socorro than to the Friscos, himself rode into Upper Frisco to speak with the justice of the peace.

After a meeting with the J.P. both men, with ten other cowboys riding behind them, went to Lower Frisco to see about getting McCarty released.

Among the ten cowboys riding with them were Dave Matthews and Rob Thomas from the Slaughter spread, and Jack Perham, the Slaughter foreman. McCarty worked for Slaughter, but Perham had not sent word to his boss because McCarty was one of the cowboys who had shot pieces off of Epitacio Martinez, and if this arrest had anything to do with that, Perham didn't want Slaughter to know about it.

Perham was going to try to handle this without letting his boss know what was going on.

"They just stood there and let you take him?" Pedro Saraccino asked Elfego incredulously.

They had just deposited McCarty in a jail cell and Elfego had hung the keys back on the wall peg behind Saraccino's desk.

"They didn't know what to do," he explained. "They had no leader."

"And when they find a leader, what will they do?" Saraccino asked.

"I don't know," Elfego said. "Perhaps that will not be until I leave with him for Socorro tomorrow morning. Perhaps by the time they figure out what to do I will already have turned him over to the sheriff."

"I hope you're right," Saraccino said.

Elfego put his hand on the deputy's shoulder.

"I told them you had nothing to do with this," he explained, "and that I was just using your jail cell."

"I am not worried about me, 'Fego," Saraccino said, "I'm worried about you."

"Let me worry about that," Elfego said. "I have gotten to be pretty good at it."

Suddenly, they could hear the sound of horses—ten or twelve, probably—coming closer.

"It looks like we're not going to get to wait until morning," Saraccino said.

Naranjo, quiet until now, moved to the window and looked out.

"Twelve riders," he said. "They're stopping right outside."

Elfego took his gun from his belt, checked to see that it was loaded properly, then did the same with the gun from his holster.

"Both of you stay inside. It's me they'll want to talk to."

"But Elfego—" Naranjo protested.

"Never mind," Elfego said. "Stay inside with the prisoner."

As Elfego went out the door, Saraccino asked Naranjo, "What did this *gringo* do, anyway?"

"He was beating another *gringo* over the head with his gun," Naranjo explained.

"Another *gringo?*"

"*Sí.*"

"Elfego could not even wait for one of our own people to be assaulted?" Saraccino asked.

"My friend," Naranjo said, with more wisdom than he usually possessed, "I believe he is trying to avoid that happening again."

"But by making an example of this *gringo,*"

Saraccino said, "he brings all the others down on his head."

"I believe he knew that would happen," Naranjo said.

Saraccino shook his head and said, "If he lives to be twenty, it will be a miracle."

Chapter Eleven

Elfego Baca stepped outside the jail and faced the men assembled on horseback. He recognized a few of them. One was a man named Wilson who had a ranch nearby; another was Perham, the foreman of the Slaughter Ranch. The third man he recognized was the justice of the peace, Lopez. He wondered what he was doing there with the cowboys. Elfego kept his right hand poised near his holster, the left ready to grab for the gun in his belt if he needed it.

"We're here for McCarty," Wilson said. He was apparently the spokesman.

"He is my prisoner."

"You have no authority."

"I am making my own."

"You're an arrogant young pup, aren't you?" Perham shouted.

"You can take this up with the sheriff in Socorro tomorrow," Elfego said, "after I deliver my prisoner to him."

Wilson opened his mouth to say something, but it was the foreman, Perham, who spoke out first.

"You're not takin' him to Socorro," he shouted. "We're takin' him back right now, ain't we, boys?"

To his credit Wilson seemed alarmed by this announcement, but the other cowboys shouted their agreement with Perham.

"I am going to give you all to the count of three to ride out of town," Elfego said.

"He's bluffin'," Perham said. "He'd never draw on all of us."

The cowboys with him seemed to agree, but both Wilson and the justice of peace—who never got to say a word—started to shy away from the potential line of fire.

"One . . ." Elfego said. "Two . . ."

"Let's take our man out of that jail, boys!" Perham shouted.

"Three!" Elfego said. He drew both weapons at the same time and began to fire. Almost immediately the cowboys scattered, attempting to dodge the bullets rather than return fire.

It was quite a sight, this young man standing with a blazing gun in each hand, no one daring to shoot back at him. They all thought he was crazy, just standing out in the open letting lead fly. For the most part Elfego was deliberately missing them, firing above their heads or between them. In one case a man named Allen had his horse carry him into the path of a bullet, which shattered his knee. In the midst of all this Perham's horse shied, reared, and then fell, landing on Perham and swiftly crushing the life out of him. By the time the shooting stopped and the smoke cleared there were only those two men left, both on the ground, the foreman dead and Allen with a shattered leg.

The door to the jail opened and Pedro Saraccino came running out. He took in the scene and shook his head. *"Madre de dios!"*

Elfego reloaded, put up his weapons, and entered the jail.

Chapter Twelve

Saraccino spent some time removing Perham's body and taking Allen over to the doctor. When he returned to the jailhouse, he found Elfego lounging in front of his desk with his heels up on it. Naranjo was standing by the window.

"Elfego," he said, "Wilson and the justice of the peace want to come in and talk to you."

"Just the two of them?"

"Yes."

"Very well," Elfego said. "Are they outside?"

"Just outside the door, Elfego," Naranjo said.

"I will see them in," Saraccino said.

He went to the door and opened it, allowing the two men to enter. They had their hats in their hands and their heads down as Elfego turned to face them. However, Elfego did not believe that they were as downcast as they pretended to be.

"What happened outside should never have happened," Wilson began.

"I agree," Elfego said.

"One man is dead—"

"I did not kill him."

"No," Wilson said, "his horse fell on him. Unfortunately, he is the foreman of the Slaughter ranch. When John Slaughter hears about this, he's not going to—"

"Is this why you wanted to speak to me?" Elfego asked, cutting the man off. "To warn me of John Slaughter?"

"No," Wilson said. "Senor Lopez, here, has agreed to try McCarty in his court in Upper Frisco, if you will take him there tomorrow."

"Is this true?" Elfego asked the J.P.

"Yes."

"You were against this earlier today. What happened?"

"I have been . . . convinced otherwise," the man said.

"So you see," Wilson said, "there's no reason to take McCarty to Socorro. After all, he's not guilty of any vicious crime."

"He broke the law."

"Granted," Wilson said, "and he should be tried here where he broke it."

"I agree," Elfego said.

"Then will you bring him to court in the morning?"

67

"We will be there."

"Excellent."

"How is the man who was shot?" Elfego asked.

"He's . . . his knee has been shattered. He won't ever walk normally again."

"I am sorry for that," Elfego said. "It was my intention to disperse the mob, not to actually wound anyone. It . . . got out of hand."

"Yes," Wilson said, "it did." He put his hat back on. "We'll see you in court tomorrow, then."

Lopez bobbed his head, put his hat on, and left with Wilson, not saying another word.

"Why couldn't they say that before?" Saraccino asked.

"They did not think I was serious before," Elfego said. "Unfortunately, this is what it took."

"I will go to court with you tomorrow—"

"No, Pedro," Elfego said, "I will do it myself."

"I can come—" Naranjo began.

"Francisco, you have done enough."

Naranjo laughed. "I have done nothing."

"Yes, you have, my friend," Elfego said, taking hold of the man's arm briefly. "You have done more than anyone else, but tomorrow I will take McCarty to court alone. It is a thing I must do."

"But I wish to help—"

"You can help by staying here in the jail with him tonight," Elfego said. "I will get some sleep and come back early to relieve you. Will you do that?"

"Yes."

"*Bien.*"

"Come," Saraccino said, "we will go home and get something to eat. Francisco, I will bring you something later."

"*Gracias.*"

Elfego and Saraccino stepped outside and stopped just in front of the jail.

"One man dead, one injured," Saraccino said. "If this was all it took to make changes, it was not too bad."

"It's not over yet," Elfego said. "Let's see what happens tomorrow. There will still be John Slaughter to deal with."

"*Sí,*" Saraccino said, "you are right."

"But first things first," Elfego said. "When the *gringos* see one of their own tried by one of our own, then they will understand that the Friscos are not theirs to ride roughshod over."

"What if he is not convicted?"

"That doesn't matter," Elfego said. "Simply that he will be tried is enough."

"Come, then," Saraccino said. "Some hot food and some sleep will do you good. You have done yourself proud . . ."

Elfego smiled and added, ". . . for a self-appointed lawman."

Chapter Thirteen

Dave Matthews and Rob Thomas returned to the Slaughter ranch to tell John Slaughter about the death of Jack Perham. The rancher listened without comment while they told him what had happened, and why.

"Why didn't Perham come to me?" he asked when they were finished.

Matthews and Thomas could only exchange a glance.

"Perham was involved in the shooting, wasn't he?"

"The shooting?" Matthews repeated.

"The Mexican man who was used as target practice," Slaughter said. "The incident that spawned this whole mess."

"Well . . ." Thomas said.

"And both of you were also, weren't you?" Slaughter asked.

Denial did not come to the men. They exchanged another glance, unsure of what to say. Neither man was the type to take the lead, and there was no one in the room for them to follow.

"Pack up your gear and clear out, both of you," Slaughter finally said.

"Huh?" Thomas said.

Matthews only swallowed.

"But, Mr. Slaughter," Thomas said, "that Mexican deputy—"

"Will be taking McCarty in to court tomorrow to be tried," Slaughter said. "Whatever the outcome of the trial is, he's fired, too. Now get out, both of you."

They exchanged yet another glance before they stood up and skulked out. Slaughter pushed them from his mind and turned his attention to finding a new foreman.

When A. C. Wilson walked into Milligan's Saloon later that night, he saw Thomas and Matthews drinking at a table. He got himself a beer and joined them.

"You two look like you lost your best friend."

"Our jobs, is more like it," Thomas said.

"Slaughter fired you?"

"Us and McCarty," Matthews answered.

"Well, don't worry about it," Wilson said. "You've all got jobs with me."

"We do?" Thomas asked.

"As long as you're willing to do what I tell you to do," the rancher said.

"Like what?" Matthews asked suspiciously.

"I convinced that Mexican deputy to take McCarty into Justice Lopez's court tomorrow morning for a hearing."

"We heard that," Thomas said.

"Well, before he ever gets to Lopez's court, we're gonna take McCarty away from him. I'll need all the men I can get."

"How many?" Thomas asked.

"He stood off twelve today," Wilson said. "I want at least five times that in the Plaza tomorrow when he shows up with McCarty. Are you boys in?"

"It's because of that Mex we got fired," Thomas said.

"And Perham's dead," Matthews added.

"We're in," Thomas said.

"Good," Wilson said. "Be in the Plaza tomorrow morning at eight A.M."

"We'll be there," Matthews said.

"That Mexican is gonna be sorry he ever arrested an American," Wilson said, standing up. "I'll see you boys tomorrow."

Wilson left and walked over to Justice Lopez's house.

Once again Elfego and Saraccino smoked cigars together outside the house after a late supper.

Carmen was much happier now that the arrest had been made and her husband was still alive. They could hear her singing as she cleaned up inside.

" 'Fego, are you sure you don't want me to go to the Upper Plaza with you tomorrow?" Saraccino asked.

"I am very sure, Pedro," Elfego said. "Carmen would never forgive me now if something happened to you. She's too happy."

" 'Fego—"

"Forget it, Pedro," Elfego said, slapping his friend on the back. "By this time tomorrow it will be all over."

"And I did nothing to help."

"Don't be sad, my friend," Elfego said. "You did what you could."

"Carmen," Saraccino said, "if I did not love her so—"

"If you love her enough," Elfego said, "perhaps you should think about moving on and finding another job, eh?"

Saraccino touched the badge on his chest. "Perhaps you are right. I am really not the man to wear this." He took it off and held it out to Elfego Baca. "But you are."

"Well," Elfego said, taking it, "perhaps just for tomorrow."

Chapter Fourteen

At 8 A.M. the next morning, Elfego Baca appeared at the jail with Pedro Saraccino. Immediately, Francisco Naranjo noticed that it was Elfego who was wearing the badge.

"My last official duty," Saraccino said, taking the cell key off the wall peg, "will be to turn McCarty over to you."

Naranjo didn't understand, but he saved his questions for later.

Saraccino went into the back and came out with McCarty, pushing him ahead of him.

"You're not gonna get away with this, Baca," McCarty said.

"Perhaps not," Elfego said, "but I am going to give it a try. We are going outside now. If you try to run, I will shoot you in the leg. Do you understand?"

"Yes, I understand, you dirty Mex."

Elfego would not be baited by the *gringo*'s insults.

Outside the jail Elfego had his white horse, and another animal for McCarty to ride. Because McCarty was manacled, Elfego helped the man onto his horse, then mounted his own. Both Saraccino and Naranjo came out to wish him good luck.

"If I have any," he replied, "this will be over soon."

He turned his horse, and McCarty's with him, and started to ride away from the jail. Suddenly, about two hundred yards ahead of him, he saw two riders. As he closed on the horsemen he recognized them as two *gringos* named Clemente Hightower and Jerome Martin. By the time he closed to within hailing distance, he had one gun in his hand.

"We're not here for trouble, Elfego," Hightower said. "We're here to warn you."

"About what?"

"There are about a hundred men waiting in a canyon for you between here and Upper Frisco," Martin said.

"Why are you telling me this?"

"Because we don't want to see you get killed,"

Martin said. "It's bad business to be killing lawmen."

"I am self-appointed," Elfego said.

"Self-appointed or not," Hightower said, "you're wearing a badge today, aren't you? Just be careful. Find yourself another route to Milligan's Plaza."

"*Gracias,*" Elfego said. "I will do that."

The two men nodded to him, then moved aside to let him by. As they passed, Elfego heard McCarty mutter, "Traitors!"

Circumnavigating the canyon added some time to the trip, but they finally reached Milligan's Plaza in Upper Frisco. Elfego saw the justice waiting for them outside his office. They rode up to him and dismounted.

"We are here," Elfego said, "as promised."

"I see that," Lopez said.

Lopez was gazing past Elfego, who turned to see what the man was looking at. Apparently, the men waiting in the canyon had gotten tired and ridden to the Plaza. As they approached, Elfego reckoned they were eighty strong rather than a hundred. Later testimony would prove him right.

Elfego turned to look at the justice, but the man had retreated into his office.

"You're finished now," McCarty said.

"If I am," Elfego said, putting his hands on his gun, "you are too."

The mob of cowboys rode toward them, and

Elfego saw Wilson in the lead. Apparently, the man had not meant anything he'd said the day before.

The cowboys stopped, but Wilson came a bit closer.

"Hello, Mr. Wilson," Elfego said.

"Hello, you dirty Mexican sonofabitch."

Elfego was about to reply when someone from the group fired a shot. The bullet whizzed by and struck the side of the building. Elfego immediately drew both guns and covered Wilson and the men closest to him.

"Come on," he said to McCarty, and the two men backed into an alley together.

"You can't get away," McCarty said, and he dragged his heels so much that Elfego had to leave him.

Once in the alley, Elfego looked around for an escape route. What he saw, in a clearing at the end of the alley, was a small building called a *jacal*. It was a house owned by a man named Geronimo Armijo. Inside, however, were only Armijo's wife and two small sons.

"*Vamos!*" Elfego shouted. "Get out. You are in danger if you stay here."

Somehow the woman must have known who he was, for as she passed him, ushering her sons out, she paused to touch his arm and say, "*Vaya con dios.*"

"*Gracias.*"

As the woman left, Elfego closed the door and

bolted it. He looked around for something to barricade it with and had to settle for a large wooden chest. Then he grabbed a wooden table to drag over to a window. He turned it over on its side to give himself extra cover, then drew both guns again and crouched behind the table.

"Now we will see," he said.

Wilson and his men came within sight of the *jacal* and stopped. McCarty had run off and was not to be part of what happened next. He was glad to have gotten away from the Mexican, and wanted only to put distance between himself and this town.

"He's barricaded himself inside," Wilson said.

It seemed to matter little to the assembled that they had accomplished their goal of getting McCarty away from Elfego. Now that Elfego had taken cover in the *jacal*, they suddenly wanted to get him out.

A man named Kearns, who worked for Wilson on his ranch, came forward and said, "I'll get the dirty little Mexican out of there, boss."

"Kearns!" Wilson shouted, but it was too late. The man was charging the small structure with his gun in his hand.

Kearns took three steps toward the *jacal* and fired one shot. From inside Elfego fired both guns, one shot from each. Both bullets found a home in the chest of Kearns, knocking him off his feet and instantly killing him.

Two men rushed forward and pulled Kearns out of the way.

A man named Jim Cook, who worked for Slaughter, came up alongside Wilson.

"He's a crack shot, Mr. Wilson," he said. "Barricaded in there like he is, he could take a few of us with him if we rush him."

"We're not gonna rush him," Wilson said.

"What are we gonna do, then?"

Wilson looked at Kearns. "We're gonna shoot that shack to pieces and bring it down around his head."

"But—"

"But what?"

"McCarty got away, Mr. Wilson," Cook said. "Why are we—"

Wilson ignored Cook, turned to the men, and said, "Take cover wherever you can and fire on my order."

The men scattered and started taking cover. Wilson turned back to look at Cook.

"We're gonna teach that Mex a lesson, Cook," Martin said. "You with us?"

Cook hesitated, then said, "I'm with you."

"Then take cover," Wilson said, "and fire on my signal."

"Right."

Cook found cover, as did Wilson, who figured they had enough guns to riddle the *jacal* with a hail of bullets that would bring it down.

"Ready . . ." he shouted, ". . . fire!"

And the fight began.

Chapter Fifteen

Actually, it wasn't a fight, it was more of a siege.

A *jacal*—pronounced "hackawl"—is a facsimile of an adobe house. However, it is not adobe, but more dried mud, and as such has little or no resistance to bullets.

Once the bullets fired by the cowboys began to whistle through the *jacal*, pieces of it began falling away. The mud and roof were held up by long stakes set two inches apart. In the first barrage some of the stakes were splintered. Elfego covered his head with his arms until the firing stopped. When it was quiet, he sat up and shook off the dried mud that had come down on him. The interior of the *jacal* had also filled with dust from the falling walls and ceiling.

While the cowhands were reloading, Elfego

took the opportunity to take a look outside to see what was what. He saw one man moving toward the *jacal* stealthily, keeping low, gun in hand. Elfego let him get close enough to encourage him, then fired one shot that killed the man instantly. Elfego vowed not to fire a shot, and waste a bullet, unless he could be deadly accurate. Picking men off accurately, one at time, would serve as a hell of a deterrent.

He allowed the others to drag the dead man away without taking a shot at them.

The siege began at nine o'clock. The cowboys fired into the *jacal* at intervals of about every half hour, stopping to reload and check for Elfego's reaction. It was not how often they fired that they thought would make them successful, but the concentration of fire when they did shoot. Eventually, they felt they could bring the entire structure down on Elfego Baca, enabling them to either capture or kill him.

Meanwhile, the word spread through Lower, Middle, and Upper Frisco that Elfego Baca was holed up in a *jacal* holding off at least eighty cowboys, most of whom worked for John Slaughter. Some of the Mexicans who lived in the area came to watch, staying well back from the action but taking great pride in the fact that one of their own was causing the cowboys all this trouble.

Naranjo went to Saraccino's house to tell the ex-deputy what was happening.

"I knew we should have gone with him," Saraccino said.

"And get killed?" his wife demanded. "What would that accomplish?"

"Elfego is not dead," Naranjo said.

"Not yet," she said, "but he is as good as dead. How can one man hold off that many?"

"I don't know," Naranjo said. "But if anyone can, it is Elfego Baca."

Saraccino took Naranjo's arm and walked him out of the house, onto the front porch.

"Keep an eye on what's happening and let me know," he said.

"What are you going to do?"

"I'm going to see if I can't raise some men—a force of some kind—to help Elfego. Maybe when our people realize that he got into this trouble by trying to help them, they'll want to lend a hand."

"How many do you think you can get?"

"I don't know," Saraccino said. "Some of the people are sick—the jaundice is among us—others will be too frightened. I don't know how many I can get, but I will try."

"You can count on me," Naranjo said.

"So far, Francisco," Pedro Saraccino said, "you have been the only one he has been able to count on."

Chapter Sixteen

The day did not go swiftly for Elfego Baca. His only consolation in the *jacal* was a three-foot plaster statue of a saint called *Mi Senora Santa Ana*. He not only prayed to the saint, but he put his hat on her head, visible from the outside, while he moved to another section of the house. He sat in a corner, resigned to the fact that he was going to be there awhile. From his vantage point he was able to watch the cowboys through cracks in the wall and keep them at bay with well-timed shots, wounding several of them as he did.

As for the cowboys, they managed to increase their cover by stringing blankets between the buildings they had hid in and around. Blankets offered no protection against bullets, of course, but enabled the men to move about between the buildings without being seen by Elfego.

At about six P.M. after a period of silence, the cowboys once again began firing a concentrated barrage into the *jacal*. Elfego threw himself to the floor, where he was lying on his stomach when the bullets managed to chew away enough of the *jacal* to bring a portion of the roof down on him. Suddenly, instead of taking cover on the floor he was pinned there by the debris. He didn't move, because the bullets were still whizzing overhead.

He looked up at the statue, impressed by the fact that she still remained unharmed. None of the bullets that were whizzing overhead had struck her and, miraculously, none of the debris had landed on her.

"Santa Ana," Elfego said fervently, "keep me safe."

As part of the roof fell in on Elfego Baca many of the Slaughter men let out a cheer, but A. C. Wilson soon cut them off.

"Stop cheering and keep firing," he shouted. "With any luck we can bring the whole thing down on him."

The eighty or so cowboys commenced firing again and did not let up.

Back in Lower Frisco, Pedro Saraccino and Francisco Naranjo met again, this time at the jail.

"What is the news?" Saraccino asked.

"It is amazing," Naranjo said. "Elfego is managing to hold off the *gringos*."

"How many of them are they?"

"Some same eighty, some say a hundred," Naranjo said. "He has killed some of them, wounded a few others. It is possible he will hold out until help comes."

"Help will have to come from outside, I am afraid, Francisco," Saraccino said.

"You could find no one . . ."

"No one," the ex-lawman said. "It seems those who are willing are not able, and those who are able are not willing."

"So Elfego is alone."

"*Sí,*" Saraccino said, " 'Fego is alone."

Both men stood and stared at each other.

"He is one against eighty," Saraccino said, "and if we go to help then we will be three against eighty."

"Not very good odds," Naranjo agreed.

They remained silent, each afraid that the other would think him a coward.

"I'll ride to Socorro for the sheriff," Saraccino finally said. "We need someone to take charge of the situation."

"Very well," Naranjo said. "I will remain here and keep a watch on things."

"I'll hurry," Saraccino said, and they both left the jail. "I will leave as soon as I have told my wife."

"Go swiftly, my friend," Naranjo said. "It is the only hope 'Fego has."

The shooting went on for two hours, and abated only when darkness fell. Only then did Elfego set about freeing himself from the debris that was holding him tightly to the floor. He worked his way to what was left of one wall and peered out through the cracks. Total darkness had not yet arrived, but the men were staying under cover of the buildings or the blankets and he could not see them. Mercifully, though, they had stopped firing, probably more because of the darkness than a lack of ammunition.

Elfego, believing that he might actually be left alone for the night, looked around and spotted the stove against the wall. He was surprised it was still standing, and when he put his hand on it he found it to still be warm. A pile of cut cottonwood sat next to it, and he tossed a few pieces inside.

For want of something better to do he made some coffee, began to fry some meat, and, in the end, actually made himself a *tortilla* dinner.

Chapter Seventeen

In truth, Elfego Baca was not hungry. He had not felt hunger throughout the ordeal in the *jacal*. He cooked and ate, though, as a sort of act of defiance against the virtual certainty that this would end with his death. He was thumbing his nose at fate.

In his mind it was only a matter of time. Either the entire structure would fall in on him, killing him, or he would eventually be disabled enough for the cowboys to come forth and do the job. To this point, however, he was not injured and—incredibly—the statue *Mi Senora Santa Ana* hadn't even been scratched.

"Santa Ana," he said to the statue, "I must trust you to protect both of us."

Then he moved the statue so that he could keep

it near him, thus making the saint's job of keeping them both safe easier for her.

Now the young Mexican sat looking outside, holding a cup of coffee in one hand. It was midnight, and he peered out into the darkness, wondering if his mind was playing tricks on him, for he thought he saw a small pinprick of light coming toward him. He wondered if it was a cowboy's cigarette that had been discarded and was now being blown about by the wind.

As he watched it would stop for a time, then begin moving again. He thought it odd that a discarded cigarette would remain lit for that long, but he did not know what else to make of it.

Out in the darkness one of the Slaughter cowboys continued his slow but steady approach to the *Jacal*. In his right hand he held his gun, and in his left he had the object that Elfego Baca was identifying as a cigarette. It was, in fact, the lit fuse on a stick of dymanite.

Earlier in the evening some of the cowhands had decided that Elfego Baca was going to continue to be hard to dislodge from the *jacal*. It was A. C. Wilson who got the idea for a couple of the cowboys to ride to the Cooney mine and pick up a few sticks of dynamite.

"We toss one or two sticks into that house and the whole thing will just blow," he said, "with Baca in it."

Two men were chosen to ride for the dynamite,

and then between them they chose which one would actually get to blow up the *jacal*.

It was a spirited discussion, as they both wanted to be the one to blow up the Mexican. In the end, though, someone produced a deck of cards. The two cowboys drew for high cards and one of them managed to come up with the ace of spades.

The Death card.

Now that man was moving closer and closer, his eyes alternating between the *jacal* and the long fuse that was slowly burning down to the stick of explosives in his hand.

He wanted very much to blow up the Mexican, but he didn't want to lose his hand doing it.

Despite what he had accomplished so far Elfego Baca was still only nineteen years old. To this point in his life he had never seen a stick of dynamite—in fact, he had never even heard of dynamite.

So he continued to watch what he thought was a cigarette blowing in the wind, moving closer and closer to his *jacal* fort.

It came as a huge surprise to him when there was a loud explosion and suddenly what remained of the *jacal* seemed to come down on his head.

Chapter Eighteen

The explosion rocked everyone near it.

It made the ears of the cowboys ring. They could only imagine what it had done to the Mexican inside.

"If he survives that," Martin said, "it will be a miracle."

"Should we go in and look, boss?" one of the men asked.

"No," Martin said, "we can afford to wait until first light. Unlike Mr. Baca, we have all the time in the world."

Inside the ruined *jacal* all was still. The statue of the saint remained standing, still unharmed. Then, slowly, Elfego began to move, to dig himself out from the dirt and debris that buried him.

His face and clothes black with dirt, he reached for the statue and stroked its smooth surface.

"My lady," he said, gratefully, "thank you for protecting me."

He dug himself out from beneath the dirt and plaster and took stock of his situation. Half of the *jacal* was in complete ruins, and the other half was a shambles. But he was still alive, and he still had cover.

He crept to the wall and looked out, fearful that he would see another small light coming toward him. He still was not sure what happened, but he did associate it with that light. He vowed to open fire if he saw another, but he did not. Apparently, the cowboys were satisfied with what they had accomplished for the night. Elfego could not go to sleep for fear that they would creep up on him, but he stayed where he was, at the crack in the wall, and dozed intermittently for the remainder of the night.

At first light a cowhand came to the corner in which A. C. Wilson had gone to sleep and shook him awake.

"Wha—what is it?" Wilson asked, staring up blearily at the man.

"I think you're gonna want to see this, sir."

Wilson staggered out of his blanket, got to his feet, and followed the man. As he came within sight of the *jacal* he was aware of cheers from the hills and the area around them. These were the

Mexicans who lived in the Friscos, the followers of Elfego Baca. In holding the Americans off for almost twenty-four hours, he already had become something of a legend to them.

"What the—" Wilson said.

"It just started, sir," the man said to him.

"How the hell—" Wilson started, but there was no point in finishing. All of the Americans were feeling the same way.

Wilson stared incredulously, along with the rest of the cowboys, at the smoke that was coming out of the chimney of the *jacal*—or what was left of it. Smoke from a stove, not an explosion.

Elfego Baca was having breakfast.

Inside the *jacal* Elfego was once again preparing food. Not because he was hungry, but for something to do, and also to send a message to the cowhands that he was still alive. He did not expect, however, to hear the cheers of the people of the Friscos. Apparently, they were not about to come to his aid, but they were willing to lend support vocally. He could not blame them for this. Had they tried to help him, they would have been outnumbered and outgunned—although not so much as he was.

Nevertheless, he was inordinately generous in his understanding of their plight.

Chapter Nineteen

Elfego's survival after the explosion that had rocked the *jacal* the night before had demoralized the cowboys. They couldn't believe his luck. How could you fight that kind of luck?

They were so depressed by this thought that they began to fire at the structure vindictively, random volleys from different clusters of cowboys who, after working each other up with their complaints and gripes, would simply begin firing on their own.

A. C. Wilson, along with Jim Cook, stood off to the side and allowed the men to blow off steam.

"There's got to be another way to do this," Cook said.

"There isn't," Wilson said. "I say we continue

firing until we bring the whole thing down."

"What if we do that?" Cook asked. "What if we bring the whole building down on him, and he still survives?"

"He can't," Wilson said. "By God, he's just a man. He doesn't have nine lives."

"Well," Cook said, "if not nine, something akin to it."

"Nonsense," Wilson said. "We just have to keep it up. I'll let the men have some fun, and then we'll organize them again. Most of these men are yours, Cook. They work for Slaughter. Now that Perham's dead, they'll listen to you. Are you with me?"

"I'm with you, Mr. Wilson," Cook said, then added, to himself, "for a little while longer."

Francisquito Naranjo was among the Mexicans watching the siege and cheering Elfego on. He was wondering what was keeping Saraccino with the sheriff from Socorro. From his vantage point there wasn't much left of the *jacal,* and yet Elfego Baca continued to survive and frustrate the cowboys. How much longer could he keep it up, though?

Even now, as he and the others watched, someone was trying a new tactic. There was a man, holding as a shield a part of an old stove, who was creeping up on the *jacal* little by little, like a turtle.

Now what would happen?

* * *

One of the cowboys had decided to take matters into his own hands. He had found an old cast-iron stove, which gave him an idea. He would take one side of the stove and use it as a shield. Behind it, he would creep closer and closer to the *jacal* until he could get a good shot at Elfego Baca.

Wilson and Cook did nothing to dissuade the man. It actually seemed like a good idea. The man almost resembled a knight from the Middle Ages, preparing to fight from behind his shield. The stove wall completely hid the man from Elfego Baca's view, and it would take a miracle shot to hit him. However, it would take the cowboy some time to cover the distance, as the makeshift shield was very heavy.

All of his colleagues put up their guns and settled in to watch his progress.

From inside the *jacal* Elfego Baca watched the steady but slow progress of the man and realized it would be folly to waste a shot on him. He could not see any part of the man at all, but he still settled down with his gun in his hand, for he felt that Santa Ana would provide him with the shot he needed. So far she had provided him with everything else, and he had complete faith in her.

So he waited and watched. He waited for the first mistake by the cowboys, he watched for the first sign of the man's head above the stove front. The slightest chance he got, he would take, realizing that if he fired and missed it would fuel the *gringos'* efforts. But if he fired and was successful, it would frustrate them even more.

And then his chance came.

At one point the cowboy with the stove piece felt compelled to take a peek and see how much farther he had to go. That was his undoing. Elfego fired as soon as the top of the man's hatless head showed. The bullet skimmed across the man's skull, leaving a bloody furrow in its wake as it continued on. The man dropped his shield and grabbed his head with both hands. Elfego could have killed him then but chose not to. He allowed the man to turn and run back to his *compadres*, and that was the last such try made by any of them.

The shot was just too perfect, and it demoralized the cowboys even more to realize that Elfego had not wasted one bullet. Every time he had fired he'd hit, somehow, while they had fired hundreds of rounds, maybe thousands, into the *jacal* and he still lived.

The barrage continued until early that evening. By then Elfego had held the cowboys off for thirty-three hours—since 9 A.M. the previous morning—and not one bullet had come close to striking him or the statue of the saint.

Everything else in the *jacal* had been hit, though. It was later decided that the Americans had fired more than 4,000 shots into the *jacal*.

The front door alone had been struck 367 times. Every piece of furniture, every piece of silverware, every dish and cup had been struck. There was even a broom in the corner with eight bullets in the handle.

But Elfego Baca and *Mi Senora Santa Ana* remained untouched.

At 6 P.M. the shooting stopped. Wilson, Cook, and the men took stock of the situation. Four cowboys had been killed and others injured. As a lawman, though, Elfego Baca would not be guilty of murder, only of defending himself—unless a court of law decided differently.

Abruptly, Cook made a suggestion that Wilson seemed in favor of.

"To justify all of this," Cook said, "I think Baca has to be captured, not killed."

"What?"

"Hear me out," Cook said. "If we can capture him and have him taken before a judge and tried, it may justify everything we've done. If we kill him we might end up making a martyr out of him. Our kind would have a rough time around here after that."

"What are you suggesting?"

"Let's send for the law," Cook said, "and let them get him out of there."

Wilson was considering the proposition and had actually agreed, when suddenly two men came riding up on horseback. One of them was wearing a badge.

Saraccino hadn't been able to find the sheriff, no matter where he looked. Wherever the man was, whatever business he was taking care of, it was not in Socorro.

Finally, he found a deputy sheriff named Ross who listened to his story and decided to return with him to Upper Frisco. It was they who rode onto the scene just as the shooting stopped.

Seeing Saraccino arrive with the law, Francisco Naranjo quickly joined them, eager to find out what was going to happen now that a lawman was on the scene.

"Looks like the law is already here," Wilson said. "At this point we can't even claim we sent for him."

"That's okay," Cook said. "Let's just tell him everything that's happened, and lay the whole thing in his lap."

"Okay," Wilson said. "Agreed."

Chapter Twenty

"Not me," Deputy Ross said.

"What?" Cook asked.

Both Cook and Wilson had filled Ross in on what was happening, and said they were willing to stand down so that Ross could go into the *jacal* and get Elfego Baca out.

To which he had replied, "Not me."

"You're the law!" Wilson said.

"After what I just heard," Ross said, "I ain't about to walk out there and get shot."

"What if one of us went with you?" Cook asked.

"What?" Wilson said. "I ain't walkin' out there—"

"All right," Cook said, "what if I went with

you, and we also brought someone whose voice Baca would recognize."

Standing nearby, Naranjo heard this and stepped forward quickly. "I will go," he said, "but only if you give Elfego a chance to surrender."

"That's what I had in mind," Cook said. "What do you say, Deputy?"

Cook, in spite of himself, had come to admire the young man in the *jacal* and wanted to try to get him out of there and to Socorro alive.

Ross looked around and then said, "Well, all right, but we get him to surrender."

"Agreed," Cook said, looking at Wilson.

"Agreed," Wilson said.

"*Sí,*" Naranjo said, "we agree, but what about all these trigger-happy cowboys?"

Ross looked at Wilson. "Nobody fires a shot at him after we get him out. I'll take him back to Socorro and put him in the new jail we're building."

"What if he tries to escape?" Wilson asked.

"If he surrenders," Naranjo said, "he will not try to escape."

Saraccino added his words to support that statement.

"That's not good enough," Wilson said. "I want guards on him on the way back to Socorro. Thirty cowboys."

"Let's see what he thinks of that," Ross said.

"All right," Cook said, "so the three of us will walk out there."

"By God, if he shoots me," Ross said, "I'm givin' up this job."

Saraccino knew just how he felt.

Elfego watched as three men began to walk toward the *jacal.* He recognized all of them and decided he would hear what they had to say. He was actually very pleased to see Deputy Ross, with the sun glinting off his badge.

"That is far enough!" he shouted when they were within hailing distance.

"Elfego Baca!" Ross shouted. "This is Deputy Ross!"

"I see you," Elfego said. "I know who you are."

"Elfego," Naranjo called, "I am here, as well."

"I see you, Francisco, and Senor Cook," Elfego said. "What is it you want?"

"We want you to come out, Baca," Ross said. "Surrender to me and I will see that you get to Socorro safely."

"If I step out of here, I will be shot hundreds of times, before my body hits the ground."

"No," Ross said, 'that's not true. I have the assurance of Mr. Wilson and Mr. Cook that no one will fire."

Wilson's assurance meant nothing to Elfego, but he put more credence in the word of Jim Cook.

"Naranjo?" he called.

"*Sí,* Elfego," Naranjo shouted back, "it is true. They will not fire a shot."

Elfego knew it would take only one hotheaded cowboy to fire a shot and kill him. Still, here was his first opportunity to escape from this situation alive.

"I will think it over," Elfego said.

"It's getting late, Baca," Ross said.

"Morning," Elfego said. "I will give you my answer in the morning."

The three men conferred, and then Ross called out, "All right, then. At first light we'll be back for your answer."

Naranjo turned to leave, and both Ross and Jim Cook backed away a few steps before finally turning.

"Shit," Deputy Ross said, "I got to stay here until mornin'?"

"He needs time to think it over," Cook said. "He has to convince himself that no one here will shoot him."

"Give him the time," Naranjo said. "He will come out."

And so they agreed, and returned to Wilson and the others.

Inside the *jacal* Elfego looked at the statue of Santa Ana. "What do you think, my lady? Should

I trust them? Walk out there after all that has happened? Hmm?"

Elfego settled down and peered out through one of the cracks in the wall. He decided that if no one tried anything he would agree to the proposed surrender—but he would add a few conditions of his own.

Amazingly, it looked as if he might actually have a way out.

Chapter Twenty-one

At first light the three men gathered again with Wilson and Saraccino, preparing to go out to the *jacal*. In the surrounding hills the people of the Friscos had gathered also, perhaps to see the final act of this play.

"What will we do if he says no?" Cook asked.

"You got me," Deputy Ross said. "I ain't goin' in there to try to get him out."

"He's got all the men spooked," Wilson said. "Goddamn the man's luck."

"He will come out," Saraccino said confidently.

"Why do you say that?" Cook asked.

"Because this is his only chance to get out alive," Saraccino said, and Naranjo nodded.

"You might have a point," Cook said.

"Why don't we stop guessing and just go and find out?" Ross said.

He, Naranjo, and Cook started walking toward the *jacal*.

Inside the *jacal* Elfego Baca prepared to greet them. Thanks to Santa Ana the answer had come to him during the night, and he was ready for them.

"Baca!" Deputy Ross called. The three men had come as close as he had allowed them yesterday, and no farther.

"I am here."

"Come out and let's talk," Ross said. "You're under my protection."

Elfego knew what that was worth. There were eighty trigger-happy cowboys waiting all around him, and it took only one to squeeze off a shot "by accident."

But he decided to comply, as a show of good faith. In this way, he was truly putting his life in the hands of Santa Ana.

"I am coming out."

When he stepped out of the *jacal* the cowboys and the Mexicans who had been waiting all this time were surprised. Although he was dirty, he was apparently unharmed.

He stepped out and immediately covered the three men with both his guns. He ignored the cries from his countrymen to make a run for it.

"Line up!" he said. "Now."

The three men complied and stood in a straight line so they could be seen.

"What's your answer?" Ross asked. "Are you going to surrender to me?"

"I will surrender," Elfego said, "but there are conditions."

The three men exchanged glances, and then Ross called out, "What are the conditions?"

"*Primero,*" Elfego Baca said, "I will surrender myself to you, but I will not give up my guns."

"I don't know that I can—"

"I assume we will have guards for our trip back to Socorro?" Elfego said, cutting him off.

"Yes," Ross said. "Mr. Wilson insisted that thirty of his men will see us back there so that you don't escape."

"*Bueno,*" Elfego said, "that brings me to my second condition. I will accompany you seated on the back of a buckboard so that I am facing these thirty men with my guns. I do not want to be shot in the back on the way to Socorro."

"I told you," Ross said, "you're under my protection, but you must give up your guns."

"Never," Elfego said. "I would rather die. Now it is your turn to think it over and get back to me."

But Ross didn't want to think it over. He wanted to get this business finished as quickly as possible. He looked at Cook.

"Why not?" Cook asked. "He could have killed us right here and now."

"All right," Ross said. "You keep your guns. I'll arrange for a buckboard. We can leave at noon."

"*Bueno,*" Elfego said. "I will wait here until that time. You will drive the buckboard up to the *jacal* and I will get in. Only then can the 'guards' fall in behind us."

"All right," Ross said. "We'll be back at noon."

The three men turned and went back to their colleagues. Elfego went back to the *jacal* and his saint.

Wilson protested, but Ross pointed out that he was in charge. He told Wilson to choose his thirty men and have them ready by noon. Naranjo and Saraccino insisted that they would also ride along, and Ross raised no objection.

At precisely noon, Ross drove a buckboard up to the *jacal.* Elfego came out, carrying with him the statue *Mi Senora Santa Ana.* He placed it in the back of the buckboard, then got in himself. He sat with his feet dangling out the back, a gun in each hand.

"*Andalo,*" he said to Ross, and he started the buckboard moving.

Within twenty yards thirty men, including Saraccino and Naranjo, fell in behind the buckboard.

Thus the procession to Socorro began and the siege at the *jacal* ended.

The Miracle of the Jacal was over.

Chapter Twenty-two

But the story was not.

Elfego arrived in Socorro as both hero and prisoner. Although the new jail was not yet finished, Deputy Ross put him in a cell there to await arraignment and subsequent trial for his actions in the Upper Frisco Plaza.

"I suppose I should be flattered to be the first prisoner here," Elfego said as Ross was locking the cell.

"You don't seem too worried," Ross said. "I heard you killed four men in that Plaza."

"In self-defense," Elfego said confidently, "and while representing the law."

"That's another thing," Ross said, pointing to Elfego's chest. "I'm gonna have to ask you to give up that there badge, as you wasn't appointed to wear it."

Elfego took the badge from his shirt and passed it over.

"When will I go to court?" he asked.

"Well, the way things are," Ross said, "I'd be willing to bet tomorrow. The law's gonna want to resolve this thing pretty quick before there's a riot."

"I will need a lawyer, then."

"Yes, you will. You got one in mind?"

Elfego shook his head.

"I do not know any lawyers."

"Well," Ross said, "maybe your friends can help you find one. I'll be back later with some food."

"Gracias."

"I'll see if I can get you a pitcher of water and a basin to wash in, too," Ross said. "You got mud and plaster all over you."

"And please," Elfego said, "see that some family gets the statue of the saint, eh? She was very good to me."

"I'll bet," Ross said. "You know there's folks sayin' you got nine lives, like a cat."

"Alas," Elfego said, "I have only one, but the Good Mother helped me keep it."

Ross shook his head and said, "I don't know what kept you safe, but it's a damned miracle you survived."

"Sí," Elfego said, "that's what it is, a miracle."

*   *   *

The word of the miracle spread like wildfire. Elfego's reputation was made, not only as a lawman but as a miracle worker and a man with nine lives. Men and women came to the jail to talk to him, see him, even touch him. Some thought that he would be able to cure their jaundice. Others simply sought to share his good luck.

That day, at age nineteen, he became a legend.

Elfego was tried twice for what happened in the Plaza, on two different charges, and was acquitted on both. First he was tried for the men he killed at the *jacal*. The most powerful testimony on his behalf was given when the door of the *jacal* with 367 bullet holes in it, was brought to court along with the broom with eight holes in the handle.

One cowboy who was present for the entire siege testified that he believed if he were to take a Colt at that very moment and fire it at Elfego Baca's chest, the bullet would never arrive. He believed that Elfego had to be in possession of magic powers in order to have survived the incident in the Upper Plaza. He thought that Elfego to have survived, was in league with either God or the Devil.

When he walked away from that trial a free man, Elfego was charged with killing John Slaughter's foreman, Parham. Once again, he was freed.

Elfego was defended by an attorney named John W. Shaw, a judge named Warren, and a man named B. S. Rodey. He was impressed by his defenders—after all, they got him acquitted—and this may have had something to do with his later being educated in law, taking the bar exam and becoming an attorney himself.

Upon his acquittal and release, he vowed to uphold the law from that day forward. He wanted outlaws to hear his steps a block away, and be scared. For now, when he walked the streets of Socorro he was looked upon with awe by Mexicans and Americans alike. Although eighty cowboys were counted that day, hundreds later claimed to have been present. History records, however, reveal that he held eighty cowhands off for thirty-six hours with only two pistols of his own.

Several days after the trial, Elfego Baca was approached on the streets of Socorro by John Slaughter.

"Mr. Baca," Slaughter said, "I want to shake your hand."

"Why?"

"You killed four of my men during your siege the other day."

"Why would you want to shake my hand for that?" Elfego asked, confused.

"Because you might have killed a lot more,"

Slaughter said. "I am impressed by what you did, sir, and ashamed that I did not come to your aid at the time."

"I had all the help I needed," Elfego said, "from *Mi Senora Santa Ana*."

"Ah yes, the statue," Slaughter said. "We have all heard the story of you and the statue. I would like to offer you a job, sir, to make amends for the fact that most of the men who shot at you during the thirty-six hours you were holed up were my men. As I said, I did not come to your aid then, but perhaps now—"

"Senor Slaughter," Elfego said, "I appreciate the offer, but I have a calling. From this day forward my business is the law."

"Well, that's highly admirable, sir," Slaughter said. "I commend you."

Slaughter shook his hand and walked on. Elfego never quite understood why the man felt the need to apologize to him. And in point of fact, he never actually accepted the man's apology. After all, had Slaughter decided to do anything at all he probably could have stopped his men well before the *jacal* was all but destroyed. Possibly even before four of his men were killed.

Chapter Twenty-three

Socorro, 1940

"Later," he told the young reporter, "I was also a top attorney, as well."

Elfego's mouth was dry from the telling of the Miracle of the Jacal. He reached for a glass of water on the table.

"Please, Mr. Baca," the reporter said, "let me get you something else. A beer, perhaps?"

"The water is fine," Elfego said, setting the glass down after taking several sips. "At my age, the beer . . . it does not stay with me very long."

"Very well," the reporter said. "That was a fascinating story, sir. It is much more than I have heard before."

"There have been many reports of the incident," Elfego said. "Some said I held off one hundred and fifty cowboys. That was an exaggeration. There were eighty, no more."

"And the siege was thirty-six hours?" the reporter asked. "I'd heard it was seventy-two."

"Seventy-two makes a better story, doesn't it?" Elfego asked. "It was reported in one place as thirty-three. Believe me, it was thirty-two."

"And the rancher Slaughter?" the reporter asked. "He really wasn't Texas John Slaughter, the famous lawman?"

"The same name," Elfego said, "two different men."

"This is wonderful," the reporter said, writing avidly in his notebook. "I mean, to have the real story . . ."

"And if that was all you wanted to hear about," Elfego said, beginning to rise, "I am also at an age when I have been up too late."

"No!" the reporter said, springing to his feet.

"Yes," Elfego said, "much too late for me."

"No," the young man said, "I meant, that's not all I want to hear. This was a wonderful story, and it is certainly the most famous, but I am sure you have more. I mean . . . this happened when you were only nineteen years old!"

"That is true," Elfego said. "I have lived a rather long and colorful life. But you said you didn't want to hear about that. You said you were only interested in the *jacal*."

"That was foolish of me. I want to hear about

it," the man said, "and my readers want to read about it. I would be remiss if I did not write about it all."

"I could not possibly tell it all to you tonight," Elfego said, shaking his head wearily. His legs were feeling weak beneath him and he needed to lie down.

"No, of course not," the reporter said, "but I can stay longer—days, if need be—to get the whole story."

Elfego thought only a moment. "Very well. Perhaps tomorrow, after the ceremony, we can have dinner. We will see how much more I can tell you then, eh?"

"Wonderful."

Elfego started to walk away, then turned and said, "Oh, and young man?"

"Yes, sir?"

"That would be dinner paid for by your newspaper, would it not?"

"Oh, yes, sir."

"Good," Elfego said, "very good. I would not want the money coming out of your own pocket."

As Elfego walked away, the young reporter took his money out of his pocket and counted it. First thing in the morning he was going to have to wire for more—and hope they would send it to him.

* * *

Elfego took the elevator to his floor and shuffled down the hallway to his door, hoping his tired old legs would not give out before he got there. It would not do for the famous legendary lawman to be found lying in the hallway.

He entered his room and immediately sat down on the bed. Laboriously, he removed his shoes and his socks and then sat there massaging his feet.

The story he had told the reporter about the Miracle of the Jacal was mostly true. At least, he had told it to the best of his recollection some fifty-six years after the fact. He actually couldn't quite remember if he had killed one man or four. He knew he was tried for killing a man named Kearns in the Plaza, and also for death of the foreman whose horse had fallen on him.

The rest of the stories, as he told them, would become clearer and clearer to him, as there would be less and less elapsed time to cloud his memories as he went along.

He didn't mind talking to the young man about his life. After all, the article was to be a tribute to him, as was the presentation the following day. And if the youngster was going to write about him, he might as well make sure the facts were all correct.

Or, in any case, as correct as Elfego Baca could recall them.

Interlude
The Life and Times
of Elfego Baca

The key and door presentation ceremony went off without a hitch. Photographers took photos of Elfego Baca standing next to the door of the jail where he'd stayed after the Miracle of the Jacal, and then the door was carried to his hotel for him. Where he answered questions about the incident.

After shaking hands many times and enduring much back-slapping, Elfego was finally left alone at his hotel. The ceremony complete, he was promptly forgotten by the town's officials, who had other matters to attend to. It was not up to him to decide whether or not he wanted to take the door back home to Socorro with him, as he would have to foot the bill to ship it.

Sitting alone in the hotel bar, nursing a beer, he realized how fleeting fame continued to be. When people discovered he was *that* Elfego Baca they made a fuss for a period of time, but in the end he was always left alone. He would end up back in Socorro, with his wife, contemplating his past.

His life had been an exciting one. It had been his goal after the *jacal* incident to enforce the law, but there were time's when he found himself on the wrong side of it. However, those were not the stories he was going to tell the young reporter from *The Albuquerque Tribune*. Much of the time he had spent in jail over the years—never for any extended period of time—he had been unjustly put there, in his view. A perfect example was his brief imprisonment after the *jacal* incident, and his subsequent acquittal on all charges. He was always acquitted, but that was not what he wanted people to read about in this tribute. He did not want to have to try to explain these things again. Of course, he would not always have the luxury of that choice.

By the time the young reporter entered the bar and spotted him sitting at a table, he had already decided what to gloss over and what stories to tell in their entirety. He knew he was nearing the end of his life, and that his legend would live on after him. This, perhaps, would be his last chance to tell it so that people would remember all the good things he had accomplished.

"Mr. Baca," the reporter said, "I'm so glad you kept our appointment."

"And why wouldn't I have?"

"Well," the young man said, "you have been very busy. . . ."

"I have all the time in the world to talk to you now," Elfego said. "I will, however, need to keep my mouth and lips wet."

"Of course," the reporter said. "I'll get a beer for me and another for you, and we can get started."

"Excellent!"

The good stories, he thought, and the way they actually happened, right from the source . . .

Elfego Baca glossed over his years as a county clerk in Socorro, and talked briefly about being mayor of Socorro when he was only twenty-one. His fame from the *jacal* incident had gotten him elected, but he found he could not achieve his goals as a politician. He served as school superintendent of Socorro from 1900 to 1901, but thereafter held no more public offices that did not involve upholding the law. He felt it was only as a lawman, and later as an attorney, that he was able to be sure that criminals "heard his footsteps."

It was while he served as county clerk that he

read law books, studied for the bar, passed, and became an attorney.

In 1904 he set up his practice in El Paso, which was about two hundred miles south of Socorro, and he remained there until 1905, when he was appointed district attorney of Socorro and Sierra Counties.

During his tenure as district attorney it was said that Socorro was one of the best cities in New Mexico. Elfego was appointed to the post in March of 1905 by Governor M. A. Otero, and removed in March of 1906 by Governor H. J. Hagerman, under dubious circumstances. . . .

At this point, the young reporter interrupted with questions.

"Excuse me, Senor Baca, but . . . were there no incidents such as the *jacal* during those twenty years?"

"There were," Elfego said, annoyed, "but none that your readers would find interesting."

"But could you explain what it was like to be Elfego Baca during that time? I mean, was it your fame that enabled you to obtain the political offices you held—county clerk, mayor, district attorney—in spite of your youth?"

"Well, obviously," Elfego said, "a youth of twenty-one is not often elected mayor—"

"And did nothing happen during your term as mayor, nothing exciting—"

"Young man," Elfego said, interrupting him,

"the office of mayor is certainly not an exciting one. During my term I had very little cause to pick up a gun. No, no, my life became much more exciting after I became an attorney, and a district attorney. . . . There was the incident with the Chinese inspector, which caused me to unjustly be removed from my post as district attorney. . . . There was the time I spent as a special prosecutor for the Sierra County Cattle Association—ah, and it was then that I met Pancho Villa—"

"The revolutionary!" the reporter gasped. "But . . . that must be an exciting story!"

"You see?" Elfego said. "Life became exciting when I was in my thirties, when I was a man. I crossed paths again with Villa when the revolution broke out; I was hired by President Huerta to defend his General Salazar against charges in the United States—"

"But this is wonderful!" the reporter said, writing swiftly in his notebook.

Elfego was satisfied with the young man's enthusiasm as it continued to build.

"I was a private detective in Albuquerque for a time . . . a *bastonero* there, also—"

The reporter looked up, puzzled.

"What is a *bastonero?*"

Elfego knew the man would like this one.

"I was the master of ceremonies at a hanging."

The man's eyes opened wider and he wrote frantically.

"Then you will want to hear about my term as sheriff of Socorro County in 1919 and 1920, as well as my job as the chief of a gambling hall police force at the famous Tivoli in Albuquerque, where I met the very well-known singer Mary Garden—"

"Senor, Senor," the reporter said, stopping him. "You have convinced me. These years sound eminently more exciting than your time as a county clerk or as a mayor. Please, forgive me for interrupting you. I beg of you, tell me about meeting Pancho Villa."

"Well," Elfego said, "that was after I was removed as district attorney for arresting the Chinese inspector. . . ."

Two
"The Million-Dollar Cattle Thief"
. . . Pancho Villa . . . The Revolution
. . . Attorney Elfego . . .

Chapter Twenty-four

In 1906 Charles V. Mallet was the Chinese inspector of Socorro County. This meant that he was in charge of upholding all of the laws that pertained to Chinese aliens living in the county. However, Mr. Mallet was not a policeman. Therefore, there really was no territorial law that permitted him to carry a concealed weapon, yet he continued to carry one.

Mallet lived in San Marcial, a small railroad town thirty miles south of Socorro. It was there that D.A. Elfego Baca had him arrested for carrying concealed firearms. Throughout his term in office Elfego had made it his business to clean up the county. That meant no drinking, gambling, or carrying of firearms.

Mallet complained that, as a federal officer, he

had the right to carry a gun. When questioned about the arrest by Governor Hagerman, Elfego explained that Mallet had been seen carrying his gun while singing in the church choir, and at dances, where there were no Chinese in attendance. He contended that he was therefore justified in having the man arrested.

Elfego Baca's detractors claimed that the D.A. had the Chinese inspector arrested as the result of a political dispute. Apparently—they claimed—Mallet had been invited to welcome the governor to a livestock meeting in Socorro, a festivity that Elfego Baca was not even invited to attend. They contended that as a result of this "affront" Elfego had the man arrested, purely out of malice.

In spite of the fact that Mallet was eventually convicted, the charge was later dismissed by a district judge, and Elfego Baca was asked by Governor Hagerman to resign.

Elfego complied, not wishing to serve any longer under Hagerman.

So much for Elfego Baca's term as D.A., during which he accomplished mostly good, but eventually arrested the wrong man.

After his term as D.A. "expired," Elfego Baca was contacted by a man named George Daring. They arranged to meet in a café in Sante Fe, where Elfego was considering reestablishing his legal practice.

When Elfego arrived, Daring was already there

and apparently recognized him, because he stood as soon as Elfego entered the café.

"Mr. Baca?"

"Senor Daring."

The two men shook hands and sat down together. A waitress came over, and they both ordered *enchiladas,* rice, and beans.

The American was a large man in his fifties, perhaps fifteen years older than Elfego. He had the girth and complexion of a well-fed man rather than a fat one. This led Elfego to believe he was wealthy.

"I've asked you to meet me on behalf of the Sierra County Cattle Association. Have you heard of us?"

"Not exactly," Elfego said. He assumed such organizations existed, although he could not say he had even heard of a Socorro County Cattle Association.

"Well, to put it simply, we're a group of ranchers who have banded together to try to solve the rustling problem we've been having for the past few months."

"And have you solved it?"

"We think we have."

"How?"

"By hiring you."

"I wasn't aware that I had been hired."

The rancher leaned forward, smiled, and said, "That's why I'm here. To hire you."

"To do what, exactly?"

"We want you to catch these rustlers and see that they're prosecuted," Daring said. "Once you've done that, we think it will send a message to other rustlers. Stay away or deal with the famous lawman Elfego Baca!"

Elfego wondered just how many rustlers that would scare.

"And for this warning," he asked, "how much would your association be willing to pay?"

"Five hundred dollars a month."

Elfego hid his pleasure well and did not give in immediately.

"For how long?"

"A minimum of three months," Daring said, "more if you need more time."

Fifteen hundred dollars minimum.

"Will you accept our offer?"

"I will," Elfego said, "on several conditions."

"Name them."

"I am my own boss," he said. "I report to no one."

"Well . . . we'd simply want to know what rustlers you have captured, who they are, where you've taken them, or what you've done with them, that sort of thing," Daring said. "But as far as *how* you do things, that would be entirely up to you."

"That is acceptable."

"And the next condition?"

"I work alone."

"Well," Daring said, "we don't expect you to

have to go up against more than a dozen or so rustlers at a time. Certainly for the man who stood off hundreds of American cowboys at Milligan's Plaza, that would be no great chore."

Elfego did not bother to correct the man by amending the number of cowboys involved in the incident at the *jacal*.

"Any other conditions?"

"I wish to be paid at the beginning of each month."

"That shouldn't be a problem."

"And I will need an expense account," Elfego said. "More supplies, ammunition, that sort of thing."

"Well . . . within reason, I suppose that wouldn't be a problem. Of course, you would supply receipts?"

"Of course." Elfego agreed to this even though he doubted he would comply. When buying bullets while on the trail of a *desperado,* one rarely remembered to ask for a receipt.

"So it is agreed?" Elfego asked.

"Agreed," Daring said.

The two men shook hands.

"When can you start?" Daring asked.

"I will need some money today so that I can outfit myself," Elfego said. "I can be in Sierra County in two days' time."

"Excellent," Daring said. He took some money from his pocket and handed it across the table. "Will that do?"

129

"For now," Elfego said, pocketing the money, "as an advance against expenses, not against my pay."

"You're a shrewd man, Mr. Baca," Daring said. "I expected to meet a legendary lawman, not a good businessman."

"Sometimes," Elfego said, "one must be both."

Chapter Twenty-five

Three months later

Elfego Baca gave the Association exactly what they asked for. Over the first two and a half months he put most of the rustlers who ventured into Sierra County behind bars. He earned every penny of his salary and his inflated expense accounts.

And then he got on the trail of a rustler named Gillette.

Gillette was smarter than all of the other rustlers combined. Elfego tracked him for the better part of a month before losing him in New Mexico when the rustler left a train that had become stuck in the snow and found another way to get back to Mexico.

In addition to earning his salary from the Association, Elfego also knew that there was a $50,000 reward out for Gillette. It was offered in Kansas City, where they were calling Gillette "The Million-Dollar Cattle Thief." His reputation spread through Kansas, Oklahoma, and New Mexico.

After his three months were up in Sierra County, Elfego negotiated with Daring and the others for a fourth. He did not want to give up the job as long as Gillette was on the loose. He also did not want to pursue him on his own without the financial backing of the Cattle Association, just in case he didn't catch him and didn't collect the $50,000.

He sent a letter to a friend of his named Charley Hunt, who ran a saloon in a Mexican town called Parral, warning him to be on the lookout for Gillette. When he received word from Hunt that Gillette was in Parral, he wasted no time getting there.

However, in leaving the United States so quickly to go to Mexico, Elfego had not checked with Kansas City to see if the reward was still being offered. So he had to send a telegram from Parral to Kansas City and wait for a reply. Meanwhile, he simply kept an eye on Gillette, who appeared to feel pretty safe in town. All he did was eat, drink, gamble, and spend time with whores, while Elfego watched. His plan was to kidnap

Gillette, get him back on American soil, and then make his arrest.

Into this situation came a man named Pancho Jaime, a Mexican bandit for the past twelve years. Jaime had driven some cattle into town, animals he had liberated from their previous owners. In looking for a buyer for the animals, he approached Elfego in Charley Hunt's saloons.

Elfego had no need of the cattle, but he did think that Jaime could be helpful in getting Gillette over the border.

As the two sat and shared a bottle of tequila, Elfego turned down the cattle but made his own offer. Jaime—who would later take the name Francisco Pancho Villa—was not yet thirty, and not yet the famous man he would become four years later.

"I need help with a certain, uh, matter," he said to Pancho Jaime.

"What sort of matter?" the bandit asked.

"There is a man in town I want to take back over the border, where I can legally arrest him."

Jaime sat back in his chair and asked, "You are a lawman?"

"Not really," Elfego said. "I am a special prosecutor for a cattleman's association in New Mexico, hired to track down and capture rustlers."

"Ah," Jaime said, with a smile that revealed several gold teeth, "you are a bounty hunter."

"You could put it that way, yes," Elfego said.

"Well, then, Senor Bounty Hunter," Jaime

said, "how much of your bounty will you pay me to help you?"

"One thousand dollars."

"One thousand American dollars? For that much money I would take Gillette, his wife, and his entire family to the American border."

"Just Gillette will do," Elfego said.

"When do we do this thing?"

"I will let you know," Elfego said. "I am awaiting word from the States before I move."

"Very well," Jaime said. "I will wait to hear."

Plans were not to go well, though. When Elfego did get word from Kansas City, it was that the reward had been lifted. Now all that Elfego had waiting for him in New Mexico if he returned with Gillette was the remainder of his expenses, as he had already collected his fourth month's salary at the beginning of the month.

Elfego was nothing if not a practical man. It served no purpose to pay Pancho Jaime a thousand dollars to get Gillette back to the United States, and it served no purpose for Elfego to even make the effort. He decided to return to Sierra County, tell Daring that he had not caught up to Gillette, and then move on. In fact, he had already decided to move his legal practice to Albuquerque and get out of the business of catching cattle rustlers.

First, however, he had to meet with Pancho Jaime one more time.

Elfego apologized to Jaime and told him that their deal was off.

"You won't pay me a thousand dollars?" Jaime asked, disappointed.

"I cannot," Elfego said, "for I don't have it."

"But the reward—"

"There is no more reward," Elfego said. "It has been lifted."

"*Caramba,*" Jaime said, "I could have used that money."

"So could I."

"Will you take this man back over the border now?"

"No," Elfego said. "There is no profit in it for me."

Pancho Jaime could understand that very well, for he did nothing that was without profit.

"Well, my friend," he said, lifting his glass, "it would have been a glorious partnership, eh?"

Elfego lifted his glass, glad that the bandit understood, and said, "Glorious!"

The two men drank and parted company after a handshake.

Elfego Baca returned to America, resigned as special prosecutor for the Sierra County Cattle Association, and did not return any portion of his pay for the fourth month. Neither, however, did he collect the rest of his expenses. All in all, he came out ahead.

But this would not be his last meeting with the bandit Pancho Jaime.

Chapter Twenty-six

It took several years for the paths of Elfego Baca and Pancho Jaime to cross again.

For three years following his stint with the Sierra County cattlemen, Elfego practiced law in Albuquerque, first on his own and then in partnership with a man named Lowell Loughery. The firm of Baca and Loughery dealt primarily with mining properties in New Mexico, which included gold, silver, and copper.

However, Elfego Baca was in El Paso, Texas, in 1911 when Francisco Modero's forces were closing in on Juarez, which was just across the border from El Paso. The revolution in Mexico had broken out the year before, but this was Elfego's first experience with it. He heard stories about an ex-bandit who was now a soldier for

Modero, named Pancho Villa. He wondered if this was the same man he knew as Pancho Jaime.

To satisfy his curiosity, Elfego rode across the border and let it be known he was looking for the rebel camp and for Pancho Villa. Soon the news spread, and Elfego was taken to the rebel camp.

He dismounted and looked around. The men he saw looked tired and beaten, but all the news he had been hearing had these rebels defeating the forces of President Porfirio Díaz. It was believed that the eighty-year-old president was very close to fleeing Mexico City and the country.

A man approached Elfego and said, "Come."

He followed the man to a campfire and there, sitting with several other men, was the bandit he had known five years earlier as Pancho Jaime, whom he had met in Parral.

"My friend!" Pancho Villa said. He rose and embraced Elfego, who returned the embrace rather halfheartedly. This was a different version of the Pancho he had met. At that time "Jaime" had not yet been thirty, had been a bandit for a dozen years, and had possessed a certain youthful charm. The stories he had heard about Pancho Villa made the man out to be not only tough, but cruel.

This man was heavier and rougher than the earlier version in Parral. The main difference was in the eyes. These were the eyes of a bandit, revolutionary, and killer, eyes the likes of which Elfego had seen on many other men—all killers.

He hoped that he was judging Villa too harshly, and that his initial observations would turn out to be untrue.

"*Hombres,*" Villa said, "this is my friend, the famous lawman Elfego Baca."

"I am an attorney now, Pancho."

"Ah, but once a lawman always a lawman, eh, *amigo?*" Villa asked. "Much like once a bandit always a bandit, eh?"

Elfego had the impression that he had walked into the middle of an argument among the men at the fire.

"But I am rude," Villa said. "This is General Pascal Orozco, commander of the rebel forces, and this is our leader, soon to be El Presidente Francisco Modero."

The two leaders rose and shook hands with Elfego, who sensed they were uncomfortable in the presence of Villa. Orozco was older than Elfego thought a field commander should be, but he had the look of a soldier. On the other hand, Modero looked like the perfect bureaucrat, a man who had spent very little time in the field. Orozco's hand was callused and worn, while Modero's was soft and smooth.

"We were just about to read something to Pancho, Senor Baca," Modero said. "Will you join us?"

"It would be my pleasure," Elfego said.

And so it was that Elfego Baca was present when Pancho Villa was read his commission to colonel in the Revolutionary Army. Modero finished reading the commission and proudly handed the paper to Villa, who could not read and did not understand it. It fell to Elfego to take his old friend aside and explain it to him.

"You are now Colonel Villa," Elfego said. "You must sign this decree."

Villa stared at the paper in his hands.

"What is this?" he asked.

"This paper is your appointment as colonel."

It took Villa a long time to scrawl the words "Francisco Villa" on the paper, and then he tossed it aside angrily.

"What good is a piece of paper!" he shouted. "All I want to do is fight."

They sat around the campfire again, and Elfego listened as "Colonel" Villa, General Orozco, and future President Modero—and his heavily bearded aide, a man named Carranza—argued over the planned attack on Juarez.

"It is the only way to drive Díaz out of the city," Villa argued.

"I agree," Orozco said. "They hold the city, we merely surround it. We must go in and take it."

"But," Modero said, "there will be much bloodshed." The thought of it seemed to make him shudder. Villa and Orozco exchanged a glance that Elfego was not sure he could read.

Obviously, they were disappointed with Modero's attitude, but he did not know what they were planning to do about it.

The argument went on for some time until at last the attack plan was finalized. Elfego felt it was time for him to go. He shook hands with Orozco—whom he liked very much—and Modero, whom he did not think very much of. Villa walked him to his horse.

"It will be a great victory!" Villa said as they walked.

"No doubt."

"The streets will run red with blood," Villa added. "I do not know how Modero will avoid it, but I am sure he will manage to get none of it on his boots."

"Pancho—" Elfego said, then stopped. Obviously, Villa did not think much of Modero as president, but perhaps that was overshadowed by his desire to get Díaz *out* of power.

"What is it, my friend?"

"Nothing," Elfego said. "I wish you luck."

"You will be our guest in Mexico City, my friend," Villa said. "We only need to take Juarez for Díaz to flee, and then the presidential palace is ours."

"I will look forward to it, Pancho."

Elfego Baca mounted and rode away from the rebel camp, fearing that all was not right among the rebel leaders, and that everything would not go quite as planned—especially for Pancho Villa.

Chapter Twenty-seven

It took three days for the revolutionary forces to take Juarez and drive Díaz out of the country. Some said he went to the United States, others that he fled all the way to France.

Elfego remained in El Paso during all this and heard how Modero had entered the city with his wife as a conquering hero, even though it had been Villa and Orozco who had done all the conquering. Nothing was mentioned about them, though, and Elfego knew that this would not sit well with either man. He was sure there would be unrest within the victors' camp, but he was shocked to hear the eventual outcome.

Word spread that Pancho Villa had angered President Modero, and that he had been executed as a result.

Pancho Villa was dead.

Elfego did his best to find out if this was true, but the facts of the execution were scarce. Modero had apparently given some official post to his elderly father, which had further infuriated an already incensed Villa, who refused to recognize the older Modero in any official capacity. Later, Elfego heard that Villa, in a rage, had physically attacked the new president and, as a result, had been arrested and executed.

However, these were just rumors.

Several days after hearing of Villa's death, Elfego was in a room at the Zeigler Hotel when there was a knock on his door. A messenger politely informed him that Colonel Villa would like to have a meeting with him.

"But . . . Villa is dead."

The messenger gave Elfego a pitying look and asked if he would come. Elfego agreed. His curiosity would allow him to do no less.

Elfego followed the messenger along the El Paso streets until, on a corner, they were approached by two of Villás followers. The two men did not say a word, simply fell into step with them.

A few blocks later they were joined by two more men. Elfego began to feel antsy and was glad he had worn his pistol.

A third pair joined them several twists and turns later, and then the entire group ended up in a dark alley, where a man waited for them.

"Pancho?"

"In the flesh," the bandit said.

"But . . . I heard you were dead . . . executed."

"Killed?" Villa laughed. "By Modero? It is not likely."

"Well, I'm glad to see you alive."

Villa put his arm around Elfego's shoulder and walked him away from the rest of the men.

"I am in need of a favor, *amigo,*" he said in a whisper.

"What kind of favor?"

"There are certain items of value that I need taken out of Mexico," Villa said. "I am watched too closely to do it myself. I would like you to come across the border tomorrow, to take care of them for me."

"Pancho—"

He patted Elfego on the chest, where his wallet might be, and said, "It will be worth your while, my friend."

"Very well," Elfego said. "I will come."

They arranged for a time for Elfego to come to Villa's headquarters. The bandit told Elfego that he would have someone meet him at the other side of the International Bridge to guide him there.

"And now I must go," Villa said. "I may not be dead now, but there are those who would like me to be. My man will see you back to your hotel."

Elfego was going to say something else, but suddenly Villa and his men faded into the darkness of the alley and were gone, leaving Elfego standing there with the original messenger.

"You are ready to return, senor?" the man asked politely.

"Lead the way," Elfergo Baca said.

Chapter Twenty-eight

The next morning, Elfego dressed in trail clothes rather than a jacket and tie, which was the mode of dress he adopted when he began to work in earnest as an attorney. And rather than a small pistol worn in the inside of his jacket, he strapped on his holster. If he needed his gun he wanted to be able to get to it fast.

He rode to the International Bridge, with every intention of crossing and keeping his word to Pancho Villa. However, when he reached it he was denied access by American troops.

"What's going on?" Elfego asked.

"You'll have to move on, sir," an American soldier told him.

"Will the bridge be open again?'

"Maybe later in the day," the soldier said.

"Right now nobody is allowed to cross."

Elfego frowned. Later in the day would be too late, and Pancho Villa would think that he had not kept his word.

He hoped that he would be able to reach Villa and convince him otherwise.

Elfego never did discover why the American troops had closed the bridge when they did. Later in the day, however, he returned and found them gone and the bridge open. He crossed but, predictably, found no guide waiting for him.

He made an attempt to find Villa in Juarez, but without actually asking for him—he was, after all, thought to be dead.

As it began to get dark in Juarez, Elfego gave up and crossed back to the El Paso side of the bridge. Perhaps Villa would once again try to contact him.

Over the next few days Elfego got the word that Pancho Villa was not very happy with him. The bandit did, indeed, think that Elfego had simply decided not to help, and thus hadn't kept the appointment. In fact he heard that Villa had put a $30,000 price on his head, payable to anyone who could get Elfego Baca back into Mexico, where Villa could get to him. Apparently, it was no longer easy for the bandit to cross the border.

If Villa wanted to be that petty and vindictive,

without giving Elfego a chance to explain, then so be it.

Soon, before he left El Paso, another messenger came to Elfego Baca.

"Colonel Villa would like you to come to his camp."

Elfego wondered if Villa thought he hadn't heard about the $30,000 on his head.

"How does Villa feel about me?" he asked the messenger.

"Oh, the Colonel, he likes you."

"And General Orozco?"

"Villa no longer likes Orozco," the messenger said.

So Villa was at odds with Orozco and Madero. It seemed Villa was cutting his ties with everyone. Elfego still recalled liking Orozco when he met him.

"You tell Villa I will see him anytime he wants to come here," Elfego told the messenger.

"But he wants to see you in Mexico."

"I am too busy at the moment to go to Mexico," Elfego said. "Why won't he come here?"

"He is afraid that someone would try to shoot him."

"He is probably right," Elfego said. "In fact, you tell Pancho Villa for me that if I see him, I will probably shoot him myself."

Elfego thought that this message would probably not get back to Pancho Villa, word for word.

This effectively ended whatever friendship had existed between Pancho Villa and Elfego Baca, two of the greatest of Mexican legends. They never saw each other again, even though Elfego continued to go to Mexico from time to time, and Villa was spotted in the United States occasionally. Villa soon became much too involved in the next revolution—and in staying alive—to worry about finding Elfego Baca once again.

Madero's reign as President of Mexico was short lived, as he was soon removed from power by the counterrevolutionary Victoriano Huerta, who, as *Presidente*, wished to reestablish Mexico's relationship with the United States. For this he knew he would need someone to represent him in the United States and, specifically, in Washington, D.C.

Chapter Twenty-nine

Nineteen fourteen found Elfego Baca in Albuquerque, not only practicing law but also working as a private detective.

He had a business card made up that read on one side: "Elfego Baca, Attorney-at-Law, License to practice in all courts from Justice of the Peace in New Mexico to the United States Supreme Court. Fees moderate."

The other side said: "Elfego Baca, Private Detective, Discreet Shadowing Done, Civil and Criminal Investigations, Divorce Investigations Our Specialty."

That year he also served as a *bastonero*. He was the master of ceremonies at the legal hanging of one Demecio Delgadillo, who had been convicted of murdering a woman. Elfego had been a witness at many hangings in his life, and his job during this one was to make sure that everything went off as it was supposed to, including both the building and testing of the scaffold itself.

He also had a printing plant in the building he owned at Gold Avenue and South Sixth Street, where he had his offices. From the printing plant he published *La Opinion Publica*, a weekly political newspaper in which he held forth on his views and beliefs.

Elfego Baca was a very busy man at this time of his life, and he was about to take on one of the biggest cases of his career.

When General Jose Ynez Salazar was arrested in America he was charged with violating American neutrality laws, as well as smuggling munitions across the border.

President Huerta, knowing that Elfego Baca was an honest and law-abiding man, a capable attorney, and a Mexican who could operate easily in the United States, sent a telegram to Elfego in Albuquerque and asked that he go to Fort Bliss near El Paso and undertake to defend General Salazar. Since Huerta was, among other things, an enemy of Pancho Villa, Elfego accepted. He completed his responsibilities as *bastonero* at the Delgadillo hanging, and passed on to another detective his one active case—following a wayward husband.

He was looking forward to taking on the

United States of America on behalf of a Mexican general.

The same day that he arrived in Fort Bliss Elfego Baca went to the office of the commander, General Scott. As the attorney for General Salazar he requested a meeting with his client.

"No," Scott said.

"No? Why not?"

"Every attorney in El Paso has been in this office since we arrested Salazar," Scott said. "Personally, I don't care a damn who Salazar talks to, but Washington does."

"Washington?" Elfego said. "You have orders from Washington not to let Salazar see anyone?"

"Direct from the War Department."

"But . . . that is against all ethical and moral codes—"

"They don't care," Scott said. "That's why they're the War Department."

Elfego was aghast, but he had something that no other attorney in El Paso had—he had A. B. Fall.

In 1912, Elfego campaigned for Albert Bacon Fall and was credited—at least partially so—for helping Fall become a U.S. Senator from the new state of New Mexico. Fall had never forgotten the help that Elfego gave him.

"General?"

"Yes, Mr. Baca?"

"Would you have any objection if I sent some

telegrams to see if I could sway the War Department from their position?"

"Send all the telegrams you want, Mr. Baca," Scott said, "just don't expect too much."

"*Gracias.*"

It was eleven o'clock in the morning the next day when Elfego Baca had an army operator send off a telegram to Senator A. B. Fall. He told the senator about General Salazar and his situation, and asked that Fall use whatever influence he had to ensure that the General would receive the defense he was entitled to.

"Where will you be when the reply comes in?" asked the key operator.

"I am going to wait for it right outside General Scott's office," Elfego said.

"That's good, 'cause I got to hand whatever comes in to the General first, anyway," the man said. "But you might have a long wait."

"That's all right," Elfego said. "Perhaps it won't be as long as you think."

The man shrugged. "Suit yourself," he said, and started tapping out the message.

Elfego's patience was legendary. He was there in the General's outer office at twelve when the man went to lunch, and he was still there at two when he returned. He was still there at three, when the General's adjutant came out and announced his name.

Elfego entered the General's office, realizing there were other doors in and out of the room.

"I didn't think you had a ghost of a chance," Scott said, tossing a telegram across the desk at him.

Elfego picked the telegram up smoothed it out, and read it. It was from the War Department, granting Elfego Baca permission to meet with General Jose Ynez Salazar.

He folded the telegram and placed it back on the desk for General Scott's disposal.

"I would like to see my client now, sir," he said, "if it is convenient."

"None of this is convenient, sir," Scott said. "I have many officers and soldiers under my command who do not like what General Salazar stands for. So no, it is not convenient to have him here. I will have someone take you over to the stockade to speak with him."

"*Gracias,* General."

"I hope to Christ you get him off my post, Mr. Baca."

Chapter Thirty

Salazar was being kept behind a chicken-wire fence in a tent next to the stockade. As Elfego approached he saw the heavily armed guards laughing, playfully pointing their rifles at Salazar's tent. It was the behavior of men under the influence of liquor, but Elfego doubted these soldiers were drunk.

He turned around and headed back to the C.O.'s office, leaving his guide flapping his arms, puzzled.

"What's wrong?" Scott asked as Elfego entered his office.

"Nothing," he said, "except you've got some trigger-happy guards down in your stockade and

I don't aim to be around when the shooting starts."

"Wha—" Scott said, and then the light dawned. "Wait here." He stormed out of his office.

When Elfego approached the stockade this time he found two very professional guards residing over the gate, and passed through with a lot more confidence that he wouldn't end up full of holes. He even gave one of them his gun to hold.

He entered the tent, and Salazar looked up at him. Once again, upon meeting one of the leaders of a Mexican revolution, Elfego was struck by the age of the man. He should have been behind a desk, not out in the field leading men in battle.

Salazar was white-haired and haggard. Being incarcerated must have been hard on him, but Elfego had no way of knowing if it was performing his duty that had taken so much out of him, or being locked up. The man's shoulders slumped and there wasn't any sign of the demeanor of a man in command.

"General," Elfego said, "I'm Elfego Baca, your attorney."

"I have heard of you, of course," Salazar said. "The President has spared no expense, I see. He went out and found the best."

Elfego sat across from the General. "I don't know if he got the best. I fear he might have been more concerned with finding someone with a high profile."

"It doesn't matter," Salazar said. "Whoever defends me has a daunting task. The Americans intend to make an example of me. In the end, I will be executed."

"Now, that is not the attitude to take—"

Salazar waved him quiet and said, "It is all right. I will be dying for my president and my cause."

"General Salazar," Elfego Baca said, "the prospect of dying a violent or unnatural death is nothing to look forward to. As far as I can see, it does no one honor."

"Nevertheless . . ." Salazar said, and stopped as if that were an explanation.

"Well," Elfego said, "I hope you don't mind if I do my job, anyway."

"Of course not," Salazar said. "I expect you to earn your fee and do your best, and I will appreciate it."

"Well," Elfego said, "perhaps we can discuss some possible lines of defense. After all, that is what you do best, isn't it? Make battle plans? After all, we wouldn't want you to go down without a fight, would we?"

Salazar regarded Elfego for several moments, and then smiled. "Exactly. Let us proceed."

Chapter Thirty-one

Elfego Baca earned his $25,000 fee just from following General Salazar to all the places the U.S. government shipped him during his internment, as well as his own travels to Albuquerque and Washington.

From Fort Bliss he was sent to Fort Wingate, which was near Gallup, New Mexico. There he was reunited with some of his people who had also been captured. After that he was sent back to Fort Bliss, and then transported back and forth from there to Albuquerque and Sante Fe, where he appeared in court.

The case dragged on, and Elfego also built up $3,500 worth of expenses.

He went to Washington and appeared before both the State Department and the War Department to plead Salazar's case. While in Washington he also testified before a committee that was looking into the possibility of recognizing Huerta as the President of Mexico.

Elfego tried to have Salazar released on a writ of habeas corpus, but Salazar's responses during the proceedings were of a nature that got the General indicted for perjury.

Salazar spent most of his incarceration at Fort Bliss, because there were rumors that attempts would be made to either help him escape or to assassinate him.

Finally, Elfego Baca was able to successfully file his writ and the local judge ordered Salazar released. However, word came from Washington, D.C., that, writ or no writ, Salazar was not to be let go.

Later, Salazar had to answer the new charge of perjury and so was transported to the county jail in Albuquerque, where he spent only four days—from November 16 to November 20, 1914—before all charges against him were rendered moot.

History is unsure as to whether or not Elfego Baca actually knew what was transpiring on that night of November 20. Elfego definitely was with U.S. Marshal J. R. Galusha and Judge George Craig when it all happened. Whether that was for the purpose of having an alibi or not is unknown.

At 9:30 P.M. that night the telephone rang at the county jail. Two deputies, named Charlie Armijo and Delores Muniz, were on duty. The call was an emergency one concerning a stabbing, asking for someone to come right away. Neither deputy was supposed to leave the jail under any circumstances, but the fact that one of them did is directly attributed to the fact that the caller was woman. A "lady in distress" call was one they couldn't ignore.

Between the two of them they decided that Muniz should go and Armijo would stay. Muniz had been gone for only a few minutes when a male voice came in through an open window.

"Stand still and put your hands up!"

Armijo immediately did as he was told. Two masked men then crawled in through the open window and grabbed the deputy. They took his guns, tied and gagged him, and then proceeded to free General Jose Ynez Salazar from the second floor.

Armijo later told officials that General Salazar came walking down as if he "expected" to be getting out. This made law enforcement think that the escape was an inside job, which led them to suspect Armijo and even Elfego Baca himself.

What is known for certain is that the escape was well planned, probably by a woman known as Senorita Margherita. Apparently, she was very skilled, very beautiful, like a Mexican Mata Hari. She apparently mapped out the escape and made the phone call. However, she was never seen by anyone. It is also apparent that the rescue was sanctioned by Huerta himself, who had all the confidence in the world in Elfego Baca and had rejected previous proposals to rescue Salazar. However, after Washington made it clear that Salazar would not be freed, there was no choice but to break him out.

Salazar and his two rescuers slipped out the open window of the jail, into a car that was waiting outside, and drove right down Central Avenue, the main street of Albuquerque. Apparently, the Mexicans had men on every corner, on the lookout for pursuers. As the car passed each corner, the men withdrew.

At 10:05 Salazar boarded an El Paso train, which left Albuquerque at 10:15. At 10:20 the other deputy returned to the prison, discovered the escape, and sounded the alarm.

Although Deputy Armijo and Elfego Baca were suspected of complicity in the escape of General Salazar, nothing was ever proved. The countryside was scoured that night, but Salazar was already on the train heading for El Paso. They apparently detrained at a small town called La Tuna, which was four miles from the border, and crossed over into Mexico the next morning.

The authorities followed Elfego Baca for weeks after that, but were finally forced to give up.

It was months later, on April 10, 1915, that Elfego Baca and five other men were indicted on charges of conspiring to remove a prisoner from

Join the Western Book Club and GET 4 FREE* BOOKS NOW!
A $19.96 VALUE!

Yes! I want to subscribe to the Western Book Club.

Please send me my **4 FREE* BOOKS**. I have enclosed $2.00 for shipping/handling. Each month I'll receive the four newest Leisure Western selections to preview for 10 days. If I decide to keep them, I will pay the Special Members Only discounted price of just $3.36 each, a total of $13.44, plus $2.00 shipping/handling ($19.50 US in Canada). This is a **SAVINGS OF AT LEAST $6.00** off the bookstore price. There is no minimum number of books I must buy, and I may cancel the program at any time. In any case, the **4 FREE* BOOKS** are mine to keep.

*In Canada, add $5.00 shipping/handling per order for the first shipment. For all future shipments to Canada, the cost of membership is $16.25 US, which includes shipping and handling. (All payments must be made in US dollars.)

NAME: _____

ADDRESS: _____

CITY: _____ STATE: _____

COUNTRY: _____ ZIP: _____

TELEPHONE: _____

E-MAIL: _____

SIGNATURE: _____

If under 18, Parent or Guardian must sign. Terms, prices, and conditions subject to change. Subscription subject to acceptance. Dorchester Publishing reserves the right to reject any order or cancel any subscription.

federal custody. One of those indicted was Deputy Carlos Armijo.

In the end the trial ended as all of Elfego Baca's trials ended during his lifetime—with an acquittal.

Chapter Thirty-two

While awaiting trial for conspiracy in the Salazar escape, Elfego Baca had supper one night with his friend Dr. Romero. They were leaving the Paso del Norte Hotel when a man came up to them, very anxious to speak with Elfego.

"Otero!" Elfego said.

"Please, Elfego," Celestino Otero pleaded. "You must come."

"Dr. Romero," the puzzled lawyer said, "this is . . . an acquaintance of mine, Celestino Otero."

"A pleasure," Dr. Romero said, but Otero did not acknowledge his greeting.

"Celestino," Elfego said, "let us go back into the lobby of the hotel and find a corner, then we can talk."

"No," said Otero nervously, "we must talk alone."

"Well," Elfego said, looking at his companion, "I'm sure the good doctor won't mind if we go up to my room and talk?"

"Of course not," Romero said.

"Do you know Marcel Andugo's café, near the International Bridge?" Otero asked Elfego.

"Of course, but—"

"Meet me there," the other man said. "It is urgent."

Before Elfego could say anything more, Otero ran off, leaving him and Dr. Romero puzzled.

"Elfego," Romero said, "what is this about?"

"I don't know," Elfego said. "Wait. It was only several days ago that I saw Marcel and he promised to pay me part of the five hundred dollars he owes me from a lawsuit I defended him against. Perhaps that is it."

"But why would that be urgent enough to send this Otero after you?" Romero asked.

"I don't know, Doctor," Elfego said. "Perhaps I should go and find out."

"I have my car right down the street," Romero said. "Let me drive you."

"Very well," Elfego said, "let us go."

Dr. Romero parked his automobile down the street and he and Elfego walked to Marcil Andugo's café. It was Sunday and the place was almost empty. A bored bartender was standing behind the bar, cleaning glasses with a dirty rag.

Elfego and Dr. Romero approached the bar, and the man paused in his cleaning. They both looked around but did not see Otero anywhere.

"What can I get for you gents?" he asked.

"I'm here to see Marcil," Elfego said. "Is he here?"

The barman leaned on the bar and tossed the rag over his shoulder.

"Mr. Andugo don't never come down here on Sundays," he said. "He always spends the day with his wife and kids."

"Two beers, please," Elfego said, and the bartender went off to get them.

"I guess I was wrong," Elfego said to the doctor. "This can't be about the money Andugo owes me."

"What can it be, then?" Romero asked. "And if it was so urgent, where is your friend Otero?"

"He's not my friend," Elfego said. "Fact is, he's not even an acquaintance. He and I are both going on trial for helping General Salazar escape."

"What was his part in that?" Romero asked.

"Same as mine, I suspect," Elfego said, "or I thought."

"None?"

"Exactly."

The bartender came with their beers, and both men nursed them along until Elfego finally started to suspect that something was wrong.

"Otero's not coming," he said, putting his mug down. "Let's get out of here."

Romero followed Elfego to the door and outside. They looked around before starting for the doctor's car.

They drove as far as the Sante Fe Railroad crossing, where they were blocked from any further progress until a train passed. It was then that Elfego saw Otero and several other men on the sidewalks across from them. They spotted Elfego in the car and started across.

"Stay in the car," Elfego told Romero, and got out to face Otero and his friends.

"What happened to you?" Otero complained. "Why didn't you come?"

"I was there," Elfego said, "and you weren't. I don't like wasting my time, Otero. What's going on?"

Otero and his friends were on the driver's side of the car. When he didn't answer, Elfego started around the back of the car to face him. As he came around the back, Otero raised the gun he had been holding, hidden by the car, and fired. The bullet passed through Elfego's coat, just missing him.

Otero did not get a chance to explain, or to get off another shot. Elfego drew his .32 Colt and fired twice, hitting the man both times in the heart. Both of his companions turned and fled after the first shot.

Elfego did not move to check on Otero. He had no way of knowing if there were more gunmen around. He hurriedly got into the car and told Romero, "Drive!"

The train had passed, so the doctor drove over the tracks and away from the scene.

"What happened back there?" he asked.

"Otero tried to kill me."

"But why?"

"I don't know," Elfego said. "Maybe he thinks I implicated him in Salazar's escape."

"What shall we do?"

"Drive to George Armijo's house," Elfego instructed. "I will call the police from there."

Dr. Romero nodded and proceeded to do just that.

George Armijo was Elfego's lawyer. When Elfego and Romero banged on the door of the man's home on West Missouri Street, he answered and opened the door immediately.

"Elfego, what's wrong?" he asked.

"I just killed a man," Elfego said. "I have to use your phone to call the police. The doctor will fill you in."

Elfego did not bother with underlings, but demanded to speak to the chief himself.

"This is Elfego Baca," he said when the man came on the phone. "I just shot and killed a man in self-defense on Sante Fe Street, near the railroad crossing. I am now at the home of my lawyer, George Armijo." He gave the stammering chief the address. "I will wait for you here."

"But—" the chief said, finally getting in a word.

Elfego, aware that he was not always the most liked of men, said, "And come yourself. Don't send some fresh young policeman in your place. I want to talk to you!"

He slammed the phone down angrily.

"Now what?" Romero asked.

It was Armijo who answered.

"Now we wait."

Interlude

1

"I feared the possibility of a conspiracy."

"And was there one?" the reporter asked.

"I can't be sure," Elfego said. "I was arrested, tried, and acquitted."

"Isn't it true that every time you were ever tried you were acquitted?" the younger man asked.

"Yes, it is true."

"And why was that, do you think?"

Elfego stared at the young man and said, "Because I was innocent every time."

"Of course . . ."

The reporter was writing in his notebook. When he finished a line, he realized how quiet it had become and looked up.

"Senor Baca?"

"Hmm?" As if taken from reverie. "What?"

"You stopped talking."

"That is the end of the story of defending General Salazar," Elfego said, "and all that came after. President Huerta paid my fee and reimbursed me for my expenses. I was found not guilty and all was well."

"Not with Huerta," the reporter said. "He didn't last much longer as president."

"That is not important to my story, is it?" Elfego asked.

"Well, no . . . but . . ."

"But what?"

The young man fidgeted.

"What is it?" Elfego asked.

"Well . . . you didn't say whether or not you actually did have something to do with breaking General Salazar out of jail."

Elfego eyed the young man for several seconds. "I had an alibi."

"Yes, I realize that," the reporter said, "but . . . you could have been in on the planning."

"That is true enough," Elfego said.

The reporter waited, but Elfego Baca did not elaborate.

"Were you?"

"That would have been illegal," Elfego said. "I was—am—an officer of the court."

The reporter looked disappointed. Apparently, he had thought he was going to get a big scoop.

"Young man," Elfego said, "you don't really expect me to admit to breaking the law, do you?"

"Well, why not?" the younger man said. "You were tried and acquitted."

"Exactly."

"So if you admit to it, they can't try you again, can they?"

"Who knows?" Elfego said. "Perhaps they'll come up with a new charge."

"But it was a long time ago."

"Not so very long," Elfego said. He took his watch from his vest pocket and looked at it. "It's getting late."

The reporter looked at his own watch.

"Not so late," he said.

"I need a nap," Elfego said. "Why don't we meet for dinner tonight?"

"All right," the reporter said. "Will you have something . . . exciting for me tonight? For my readers?"

Elfego stood and looked down at the man.

"How exciting do you mean?"

"Well . . . we've talked all afternoon mostly about you being a lawyer," the man said, "but you did wear a badge again after that, didn't you?"

"I was a lawyer and a lawman at the same time on several occasions," Elfego said. "Once I was once even the chief of a gambling hall police force."

"Yes, you mentioned that yesterday," the reporter said. "That was when you met Mary Garden?"

"Oh, yes," Elfego said, "and Numero Ocho."

"That's number eight, isn't it?"

"Very good."

"Was that . . . a person?"

"Yes, indeed," Elfego said, "Numero Ocho was, indeed, a person."

"Who was he? What did he—"

"This evening," Elfego said, waving a hand wearily, "there will be time for that this evening. Right now I need to go to my room and contemplate my door."

"Your . . . door."

"Yes," Elfego said, "the presentation."

"Oh, the jail door you received today. I'm sorry, I thought you meant . . . Well, never mind."

"That I was going to my room to stare at my door?" Elfego said. "That would make me senile, I think. No, I must decide if I want to take my door home with me, and if so, how to get it there."

"Well . . ." the reporter said, standing up. "Until later this evening, then."

"Until then," Elfego said.

"Um . . . there is one more thing, sir," the reporter said, "if you don't mind."

"Yes?"

"I understood that you met Billy the Kid when you were younger."

"Billy," Elfego said, "yes, that is so."

"Could you tell me that story this evening?"

Elfego frowned. He had left that story out for two reasons, one being that he did not think it particularly interesting.

"I mean, I've heard how you met Pancho Villa. I really would like another story of another famous man—an outlaw like Billy."

"Billy was no outlaw when I met him," Elfego said. "In fact, it was before he became quite so famous."

"I think my readers would really like to read about that meeting."

Elfego nodded and said, "Very well, I will think about it. We were both very young, then, and it really was not . . . all right, yes. I really have to go now, though. I'm quite tired."

"Yes, of course. I'll see you down here for dinner at, say, seven?"

That would give him several hours to nap.

"Yes, all right," Elfego said. "At seven."

As he had the night before, he sat on the bed and wearily pulled off his shoes. He contemplated napping with them on—after all, he was going to have to don them again for dinner—but decided against it.

He lay down on the bed and stared at the ceiling. Telling the stories about Villa and Huerta and Salazar had brought back such wonderful feelings. He hated being old, wished he were young enough to be adding new chapters to his life rather than relating old ones.

Billy the Kid.

Wiliam Bonney.

That one could be told very quickly, he thought, yawning. There really was not much to their time spent together—nothing exciting, anyway.

Maybe he could just think of some way to make it more interesting than it was.

Not too exciting, though. After all, this was his legend.

Interlude

2

"Billy was about seventeen years old when I met him," Elfego said. "I was all of sixteen. We were both cowboying during a roundup at a ranch called La Parida Ranch. He spoke good Spanish, I spoke hardly any at all."

"But you're Mexican," the reporter interrupted.

"I was born in New Mexico, and spoke mostly English for my early years," Elfego said.

He had come down to dinner with his Billy the Kid story prepared.

"If I am going to tell this story, you cannot interrupt," he told the reporter.

"Sorry," the younger man said, "go ahead, please."

"As I said, Billy and I were cowboying, but this one day we decided to go into Albuquerque, not to look for trouble, but of course we were both very young, and we had guns, and we had wild oats, and trouble just naturally found us. . . ."

"Billy and I stabled our horses outside of Albuquerque at a village called Isleta and walked into town. It was cheaper to stable the horse there with the Pueblo Indians.

"We went to Old Town, where the Martinez Bar was. In those days the Martinez was real famous, from El Paso to Denver. It was a rough place, but me and Billy thought we could handle it.

"Well, we walked in and right away Billy figures out a way to get both the men and the women to like us. He walks over to the piano and starts playing. I didn't even know he knew how to play the piano, but he knew real good.

"When he finished playin', we walked to the bar and had a drink. While we had our drink we noticed the bouncer in the bar tossin' a few folks out when they got too rowdy. He was a big fella with a mustache, real hard-lookin' and good at his job.

"But aside from the bouncer throwin' a couple of fellas out, the place was quiet, kind of boring, so we moved on. We hit some other saloons, and had somethin' to eat, and then came back, figurin' there'd be more excitement.

"The place was crowded and the bouncer had a keen eye on things, but Billy got playful. See, he had this gun with a short barrel that looked more like a toy than anything else. So he pulls out his gun and fires it three times into the air to liven things up in the Old Martinez Bar.

"Billy told me he was going to fire the shots, but nobody else knew that it was him, and I didn't see what he did with the gun afterward. The reaction, however, was very satisfying to Billy. It got very quiet in the saloon. Bartenders dropped glasses, patrons ducked under tables, and Billy and I just stood there calmly.

"The bouncer was good at his job, though. He came right over to us and asked if we fired the shot. He checked my gun and found that it had not been fired. 'Who fired those shots?' he asked.

" 'What shots?' Bill replied.

" 'You know what I'm talkin' about,' the bouncer said.

" 'I don't even have a gun,' Billy said.

"It was true Billy wasn't wearing a gunbelt, but I knew he had that funny little gun.

" 'Go ahead and search me,' Billy said.

"Well, the bouncer went ahead and did that, searching Billy up and down and not findin' a gun. He even searched inside Billy's boots, and did not find a gun.

"Grumbling, the bouncer had to admit that he couldn't find a gun, but he was still suspicious of Billy.

" 'No offense,' Billy said, 'let me buy you a drink.'

" 'Go to hell,' the bouncer said, and walked away.

"The bouncer walked away and business went back to normal in the saloon. Billy and I started to walk around, watching some of the games. When we stopped to watch a hand of poker, I suddenly felt cold steel in my side. It was Billy's gun.

" 'Where'd you have that gun?' I demanded.

"Billy shushed me and proceeded to fire three more shots into the air, with the same results. People scattered, and it got real quiet.

"The bouncer came right over to us and stood in front of Billy.

" 'That's it. Get out!' he yelled.

" 'Why?' Billy asked.

" 'Why? For shootin' your damn gun in here!'

" 'I don't even have a gun,' Billy said.

" 'You ain't gonna fool me no more!' the bouncer shouted. 'Get out!'

" 'Now wait,' another man said. 'If'n the boy ain't got a gun, you cain't throw him out of here.'

"So they searched Billy again, high and low, and could not come up with a gun. I didn't even know what he'd done with it.

"By this time Billy had a whole gang of supporters and there was nothin' the bouncer could do about it. He gave up and went back to his post once again.

"Billy and I stayed in the Old Martinez about another half hour before we left for good. By this time I was bustin' to know what he did with the gun every time the bouncer searched him.

" 'Where's the gun?' I asked when we got outside.

" 'Here,' Billy said, and with a flair he took off his Stetson and tossed me the gun. I caught the stumpy little thing. It made a loud enough noise when it was fired, loud enough for the whole saloon to hear, but it was small enough to hide in his hat.

"Only Billy the Kid—or me—would have the speed to fire that gun three times, and then get it hid under his hat before anyone could see him, and frustrate the hell out of that poor bouncer."

"That was it?" the reporter asked. "That was your Billy the Kid story?"

"I told you it wasn't exciting," Elfego said. "Billy didn't get involved in that whole Lincoln County thing until well after that. He was *called* Billy the Kid when I knew him—although I called him Billy Bonney—but he didn't *become* Billy the Kid until later."

The reporter made a few more notes and then looked at Elfego expectantly.

"The best stories don't always involve famous people," Elfego said.

"I realize that now," the younger man said.

"Are you ready to hear some good stories about me when I was a lawman?"

The reporter took out a new pencil, turned to a blank page in his notebook, and said, "I am very ready, Senor Baca."

Three
Yours truly, Elfego Baca . . .

Chapter Thirty-three

Elfego Baca was fifty-five when he was elected sheriff of Socorro County in 1919. He was not an imposing figure, for he now had a belly and most people noticed the twinkle in his eye. To some, he even looked like someone's amiable grandpa. However, the people still respected his legend, especially in Socorro, where the story of the Miracle of the Jacal continued to be told.

During his first week in office, Elfego made it clear that he aimed to clean up Socorro. He submitted a list of criminals to the courthouse and, in due time, the grand jury handed down indictments, and warrants were sworn out and delivered to his office.

His deputies—all friends of his—were excited to go out and serve the warrants, but in the midst of their excitement Elfego Baca was as calm as could be.

"Be still," he told them. "You'll be doing your duty in due time. Now, get out of my office and send in the chief clerk."

The deputies left and the clerk entered.

"Take this letter," he told the man, who sat down with pencil and pad. " 'Dear Sir, I have a warrant for your arrest. Please come to my office by March 15 and give yourself up. If you do not I will know that you are resisting arrest, and when I come to get you I will feel justified in shooting you on sight.' Sign it, 'Yours truly, Elfego Baca, Sheriff.' "

He passed a list of names across the desk to the clerk. It was the list of everyone who'd had a warrant sworn out against them.

"Send a letter to everyone on that list."

"Yes, sir," the clerk said, his eyes wide. He wondered how many of the men would actually come in and give themselves up. Then he thought if he ever received such a letter from Elfego Baca, he would certainly give himself up rather than get shot.

He left the office and showed the letter to the deputies gathered outside around his desk.

"Is he serious?" one of them asked.

"Elfego Baca is always serious," the clerk said. "Now all of you find something to do. I have work to do."

The deputies looked at each other.

"We have nobody to arrest yet," one of them said.

"Unless we find somebody breaking the law," a second said.

"Well, we're not gonna see that in here," the third said. "Let's go . . . make some rounds."

The three deputies left, and the clerk sat down to write the letters.

Over the course of the next week, once the letters were all delivered, men began showing up at the jail and asking for Elfego Baca. When the clerk told Elfego that a man was there to see him, the sheriff came out.

"Hello, Mr. Baca," the man said. "I am here."

There were no harsh words spoken, and the men were taken to their jail cells to await their trials. For the most part the crimes they were wanted for were not serious, and they were either released after the time they had already served, or fined.

Almost everyone came in that easily . . . except for a fellow named Art Ford.

Mr. Ford decided that he would send his own written message back to Elfego Baca. It said: "If you want me, you goddamned Mexican, you can come and get me. I will be under the big cottonwood by the river at noon Wednesday." Of course, almost every word of it was misspelled, but the gist of the note was clear.

* * *

"*Cabrone!*" one of the deputies said on Wednesday. "Surely you do not intend to meet him."

"But of course I do," Elfego said. "After all, I have been invited, haven't I?"

"But, Elfego—"

"Mr. Ford did not invite you," Elfego told the deputy, "he invited me. You stay here with the others. I will go and bring Mr. Ford back."

"Or kill him."

"That," Elfego Baca said, "will be his choice."

Chapter Thirty-four

Elfego went home at eleven o'clock to see his wife, Francisquita. They had met after the incident of the *jacal* when she was sixteen and he was on trial. He proposed marriage to her very impulsively and she told him that she would marry him—if he was acquitted. Now, all these years later, they were still married, with five grown children, a boy and four girls—all of whom had moved away to live their own lives.

As Elfego entered their small house, his wife looked at him in surprise.

"And what brings you home so soon?"

"I just wanted to stop in and see my young bride," Elfego said, taking her by the shoulders. "Is there anything wrong with that?"

Francisquita giggled like a girl and laid her head on her husband's chest.

"Not so young anymore," she said.

"Younger than I am," he said, holding her tight.

They stood that way for a few moments, and then she asked, "You are going after someone?"

"Yes," he said, "but he is harmless."

"He did not respond to your letter?"

"He did," Elfego said, "with a letter of his own."

"Which said?"

"Come and get me."

She stood back and looked at him.

"So take a deputy with you."

"I don't need a deputy."

" 'Fego," she said, "you are not so young anymore, either."

"I don't need to be reminded of that," he said, "but I am still of an age to do my job."

In point of fact, Francisquita had not wanted her husband to take the job as sheriff of Socorro. She much preferred to think of him in court rather than out looking for some criminal, with both of them wearing guns.

"Don't worry," he said. "I will be back in a little while."

"If you are not worried, why did you come home?"

"Because I will be meeting the man at twelve,

and I had time to come home and tell my wife I love her."

" 'Fego—"

He held up his hand to stop her.

"We will not argue," he said. "I will be back."

"You better be," she said. "I am making your favorite dinner tonight."

He squeezed her hands. "I would not miss that," he said, and left to keep his appointment.

Elfego rode his horse to the river and dismounted a ways from the cottonwood. He decided to walk there and try not to give Ford any advance warning that he was approaching—although it really didn't make much difference, since he was exactly on time.

He tied his horse and started walking toward the clearing where the cottonwood was. He kept alert, just in case Ford was not as harmless as he thought. He'd met the man once or twice, even had him in the jail, and knew him to be a blowhard and a braggart, but not much for taking action. Writing that note was just the kind of thing a man like Art Ford would do, trying to get under Elfego's skin.

He hadn't succeeded. Elfego had reacted very calmly to the note. The only thing that would anger him was if Ford tried something stupid.

When Elfego reached the cottonwood, there was no one there. He searched the ground for tracks and there were none. Ford either had not arrived, or he wasn't coming.

Or he was hiding somewhere to ambush Elfego Baca. Killing Elfego would certainly give the man a reputation, even if it was done from hiding, but Elfego still did not believe that Art Ford had this in him.

He chose a large rock and sat down to wait.

He gave Ford an hour, and at precisely one o'clock walked back to his horse, mounted up, and rode back to town. He put his horse up at the livery, thought about going home first, but then decided to go back to his office. He didn't like telephones, but he had one in his office and Francisquita had wanted one for their house, so he'd be able to call her and tell her that he was all right.

As he entered the office, the clerk got up from his desk and ran over to him.

"There's a man here to see you."

"Where?"

"I put him in your office."

"Why did you do that?"

"Because," the clerk said, "he was making me nervous out here."

"All right," Elfego said. "I'll see to him."

Elfego opened the door and entered.

When he went home that night for dinner he told his wife, "Ford was just sitting there, already unarmed."

"What did he say?"

"He apologized for his letter," Elfego said.

"Why did he write it?"

"He said he didn't stop to think first."

"Foolish man," she said.

"Yes," Elfego said, "very foolish."

Dinner was especially good that night.

Chapter Thirty-five

Several months later, Sheriff Elfego Baca returned from Albuquerque to find all of his jail cells full.

"What's been going on?" he asked his clerk.

"New law," the clerk said. "It's called the Debt Contract Law."

"Debt Contract?"

"It makes failure to pay a debt a jailable offense."

"So all of these prisoners have failed to pay their debts?"

"That's right."

Elfego shrugged. If it was the law, it was the law.

Several days later, Elfego was standing by the clerk's desk when dinner came for the prisoners.

Usually, their dinners were brought over from the Chinaman's Restaurant, and on this night they were all being brought at once. Several waiters went in and out until all of the prisoners had been fed.

When all the waiters had gone, one last one came to Elfego with a piece of paper.

"What's this?" Elfego asked.

"You must sign for dinners," the Chinese waiter said, "or we no get pay."

Elfego took the bill, looked at the sum at the bottom, and raised his eyebrows. He signed the check, wondering how much longer the county could go on paying to feed all these prisoners.

When the waiter was gone, Elfego started trying to find the files that would tell him what each prisoner's debt-related offense was. He was in the middle of doing that when the clerk returned from his dinner break.

"What are you looking for, Sheriff?" he asked.

"The files on the prisoners," Elfego said. "I want to see exactly what they are all in for."

"I'll bring them into your office."

"Just have them ready on your desk," Elfego said. "I'll take them with me when I go *home*."

"Yes, sir."

When Elfego came out later to go home, the files were stacked on the corner of the clerk's desk. He picked them up, tucked them beneath his arm, and headed for home.

*　　*　　*

It was quite late when Francisquita Baca came into the kitchen. Her husband had the files spread out over the table.

"It is late, 'Fego," she said. "Come to bed."

"This is amazing," he said.

"What is?"

He looked up at her.

"I have prisoners in my jail who are there for failure to pay an eleven-dollar debt."

"Eleven dollars?"

"And they are serving sixty days. It is costing the county more than that every week to feed these prisoners," he said.

"How can they repay the debt if they are in jail?" she asked.

"Exactly!"

"And this is a result of the new law?"

"The Debt Contract Law," Elfego said. "Yes. It is a foolish law."

"But it is your job to uphold it."

"It's also my job to make sure the county does not go broke feeding prisoners," he said.

"No," she said, "it's not."

"Well," he said, scowling, "it should be."

"Worry about it tomorrow, 'Fego," she said. "Come to bed."

"I will come to bed," he said, "but by morning I will have a solution to this problem."

And he did.

When he awoke the next morning, Elfego

knew exactly what he had to do. When he arrived at his office, he told the two deputies there to bring the prisoners to his office.

Minutes later, the eleven prisoners were standing facing his desk. He spoke to each of them in turn and discovered that they all intended to pay their debts as soon as they could, and they all had families waiting anxiously for them to return home.

Elfego had them returned to their cells, then went to the courthouse to research this new law. He discovered that the law had been pushed through by prominent sheepmen in the area, and was being enforced just to keep them happy.

He returned to his office and had the deputies once again bring the prisoners to his office.

"I will make you all a bargain," he said. "You must pay off your debts or I will personally come and get you and bring you back here."

The men all agreed that they would pay as soon as possible.

"Do it sooner," Elfego said. "I don't know how long I will be able to stall before I have to come and get you. *Comprende?*"

Yes, they all understood.

"Now go," Elfego said. "Go home and go back to work. You'll only eat us into the poorhouse staying here."

The prisoners filed out past the startled deputies.

*   *   *

195

The news was quick in getting around, and very soon the phone on Elfego's desk rang.

"Hello, Elfego?" It was the voice of Harry Owens, the district attorney.

"Yes."

"It's Harry Owens."

"I know."

"Eh, how are you?"

"Fine."

"And how are your, uh—how are things at the jail?"

"Fine."

"And the prisoners?"

"Fine."

"Eh, Elfego, uh, how many prisoners do you have now?"

"None."

"Um, well, Elfego . . . you have none?"

"That's right."

"You can't have none."

"Well, I do."

"But . . . what happened to them?"

"I let them go."

"You let them . . . uh, why?"

"They ate too much."

"Ate too much?"

"Yes."

"And you let them go?"

"Yes," Elfego said, "and I won't let them back in."

"Well, Elfego . . . uh, this is very serious. . . ."

"You are right, Harry," Elfego said. "It is very serious. Do you know how much it was costing the county to feed those men each week?"

"Well—"

"And they were going to be here sixty days!"

"Well—"

"The county would have gone poor feeding them, Harry," Elfego said, "and it would have been your fault."

"My fault?"

"I've saved you from some embarrassment, and if I was you I'd talk to some of the district judges about this new debt law. It will put the *county* in debt."

"Hmmm," Harry Owens said, and hung up.

It was not long after that the district judges decided that the Debt Contract Law was a poorly advised one and it was repealed, thanks to Elfego Baca.

Chapter Thirty-six

In all the time he was sheriff of Socorro County there was only one escape from the jail—and even that Elfego Baca handled in his own way.

Two cowboys named Watson and Fisher were sharing the same cell. The jail had a newly built kitchen, and when there was a prisoner who knew how to use it, he was made the cook. One day, when the prisoner who was the cook was released, Watson managed to convince the jailer he knew how to cook. The jailer let Watson go to the kitchen, whereupon he promptly disappeared from the building altogether.

When Elfego Baca returned to the jail, he was informed of the escape. He had the jailer bring the other man, Fisher, to his office.

"Fisher," he said, "I want your help."

"With what, Sheriff?" Fisher asked nervously.

"I want you to help me catch Watson."

"Me?" Fisher asked. "How am I supposed to do that?"

"You should have some idea where he went," Elfego said. "After all, you helped him plan his escape. You vouched for the fact that he could cook."

Suddenly, Fisher became angry.

"Sure, I helped him, and then the dirty sonofabitch left me behind."

"Well, I tell you what," Elfego said. "Come and have supper with me and we'll talk about it some more."

Elfego took Fisher to the Chinaman's, where they had steaks and talked about Watson.

"I'll tell you what," Elfego said after they'd finished their steaks. "Why don't you go and bring the *hijo de un cabrone* back yourself."

"How am I supposed to do that?"

"He'll think that you escaped, and before he knows what's going on you'll get the drop on him. I'll give you a deputy's badge, a gun, a horse, and seventy-five dollars."

Fisher frowned and stared at Elfego.

"Why are you so sure that I'll come back?" he asked.

"Because if you don't," Elfego said, "I'll have to come and get you. *Comprende?*"

"*Comprende,*" Fisher said, looking away.

"When you get back I'll see to it that you get

the rest of your sentence commuted," Elfego said. "You'll be free to go."

"*Gracias,* Sheriff," Fisher said, although he thought he had very little to be thankful for.

The next morning, Elfego furnished Fisher with everything he said he would and the man set out on the trail of his former cellmate, Watson.

Elfego had no idea that he was in for one of the worst weeks of his life.

Chapter Thirty-seven

After only a couple of days Elfego began to have second thoughts about what he'd done. He had a dream one night that Fisher had found Watson and that the two had had a high old time on the seventy-five dollars Elfego had given Fisher. When he awoke the next day he felt it necessary to go and talk to Judge Mechem about his method of bringing back an escaped prisoner.

"Let me get this straight," the district judge said. "You gave this fella a badge, a gun, a horse, and seventy-five dollars?"

"Yes, sir."

"And you expect him to come back?" The judge started to laugh.

"Yes, sir, I do," Elfego said, "and if he doesn't I'll turn in my badge and resign."

The judge stopped, laughed, and said, "Believe me, Sheriff Baca, if he doesn't come back you won't have to resign."

"It's gonna work out fine," Elfego said, with more confidence than he felt.

"It's worked out well for Fisher," the judge said. "He's got your seventy-five dollars."

Elfego stood up and readied to leave the judge's office.

"Keep me informed, Sheriff," Judge Mechem said. "If your prisoner doesn't return you'll not only lose your badge, you'll finish out his sentence."

"I understand," Elfego said, and left.

It was a long week for Elfego Baca. Someone had taken to calling him on the phone in his office at the start of each day.

"Heard anything from Fisher?" the voice asked the first time.

"I don't expect to," Elfego said. "I sent him out to do a job, not to write to me."

On the second day the joker said, "Still nothing from Fisher, Sheriff? Should be hearing something soon, should you—if at all?"

Elfego kept his temper in check and simply said, "Nope," and hung up.

Before another call could come in, Elfego went to Sante Fe to get away from the joker. It was at the behest of his wife, who could see that her husband was becoming more and more worried about Fisher returning.

"Why not take a trip, just for a few days?" she suggested.

"If I stay longer and get more calls," Elfego said to his wife, "I fear I will track the callers down and—"

"Perhaps to Sante Fe? Do some shopping," she said, cutting him off. "Buy your wife a nice present."

Elfego hugged his wife and said, "Only if you come with me."

And so they went shopping. . . .

It was there that he finally received a telegram from Fisher. It was a long message, which Elfego had to pay for by the word. By the time he finished reading, he was $8.75 poorer for the experience.

In his telegram Fisher related his entire experience in tracking Watson down. He told Elfego how Watson had first looked when he found him, how surprised he had been to see Fisher.

He told Elfego what he said, what Watson said, how shocked Watson had been when he got the drop on him, the names Watson had called him when he showed him the badge and took him into custody.

He also made sure that Elfego Baca knew how Fisher had acted with bravery and skill in capturing Watson.

And in the end he asked, "What should I do with him?"

"What should he do with him?" Elfego repeated, looking across the table at his bemused wife. She could see how relieved her husband was to have heard from the man—even for $8.75.

"What will you tell him?" she asked.

"What else can I tell him?" he asked. He produced a pencil and a piece of paper and wrote his reply: "Kiss him twice and bring him in, you damn fool!"

Chapter Thirty-eight

The most notorious of all the men Elfego Baca dealt with during his tenure as sheriff of Socorro was Jose Garcia. He had killed a man in the town of Belen and taken his wife. However, since the murder of her husband had been her idea, no one was really concerned about the woman until a few weeks later, when she was found in pieces.

Some shepherds had come across a woman cut into four parts and hung from four different tree limbs. Eventually, the woman was identified as Jose Garcia's most recent romantic conquest. Apparently, he'd grown tired of her and had gotten rid of her in the only fashion he could think of—or, perhaps, enjoyed.

In point of fact, finding Jose Garcia had been Elfego Baca's greatest challenge as a lawman, as the double murderer's trail grew cold and faint. Still, Elfego did not give up and spent three months trying to find the man and was eventually successful.

However, finding Garcia and bringing him in were going to be two very separate things.

Elfego Baca's three-month search for Jose Garcia took him to Sandoval County. He heard that the man was working for a sheep outfit that was noted for hiring men who were on the run from the law. This meant that all his *compadres* were willing to shoot on sight anyone they saw wearing a star.

Elfego rode to the town of Bernalillo, which was the county seat of Sandoval County. Just outside of town he took off his badge and put it in his shirt pocket. Only then did he ride into town.

Without his badge Elfego Baca, almost fifty-five years of age, was unremarkable to look at, unless you looked closely into his eyes. Riding down the main street of Bernalillo, though, he did not attract much attention.

He rode to the livery to put up his horse, then walked with his rifle and saddlebags to the nearest hotel to get a room.

"A little old to be ridin' the trail, ain't ya?" the young desk clerk asked as he checked in.

"Old enough to do whatever I want," Elfego replied. "Key, please."

The clerk was about to make another comment about Elfego's age when he looked into his eyes. He decided to keep his comments to himself after that, and handed Elfego a room key.

"*Gracias.*"

"Sure, friend."

Elfego went up to his room to stow his saddle-bags and rifle. Before leaving he checked his Colt to be sure it was loaded, then slid it back into its holster. Although he didn't know anyone in Bernalillo, there was always the chance that someone would know him. He had to be ready for the possibility that if he was recognized, somebody might try to make trouble.

He left the hotel and went to the nearest saloon to have a beer.

The saloon was quiet, as it was midday. Elfego nursed a beer at the bar, keeping an eye out for a likely assistant. He was starting to formulate a plan for getting Jose Garcia away from his sheep-herding partners, but he was going to need help. What he needed was someone who knew every inch of the county.

"Another?" the bartender asked.

"No, *gracias,*" Elfego said. "I am looking for a place to eat, and a guide."

"A guide to take you somewhere to eat?" the bartender asked.

"No," Elfego said, "first I will go and have something to eat, and then I will need a guide."

"What kind of guide?"

"Someone who knows the area very well."

The bartender rubbed his hand over the five- or six-day growth on his jaw.

"I guess the one who knows the area best is young Alfredo Montoya," he said finally.

"How young?"

"Sixteen," the bartender said, "but on his own and able to take care of himself. For a sixteen-year-old, he seems much older."

"Where can I find this Montoya?"

"He is always around town," the bartender said, "and always looking for work."

"Well," Elfego said, "if you see him, tell him I will give him some work."

"I will tell him," the bartender said. "What is your name?"

Elfego hesitated, then said, "Bonney."

"Just Bonney?"

Elfego smiled and said, "Just Bonney."

He was able to use the name of his very old friend, because no one would ever mistake him for Billy the Kid.

"Then I will tell him."

"I am at the hotel down the street," Elfego said, "but I'll be back here this evening."

"I will tell him."

Elfego turned to leave, then said, "Oh, yes, a place to eat?"

"There is a café up the street, two blocks. You cannot miss it," the man said.

"Does it have a name?"

"There is just a big sign outside that says 'Café'."

"Thank you," Elfego said.

"Try the stew!" the bartender yelled as he went out.

Elfego waved and allowed the batwing doors to swing shut behind him.

Chapter Thirty-nine

Over supper Elfego was feeling the aches and pains of being in the saddle for months. The clerk at the hotel was probably right, he was too old to be hitting the trail. After he brought Jose Garcia back he was going to leave tracking outlaws and wanted men to his deputies.

But who was he kidding? When it came to pursuing dangerous men, he trusted no one as he trusted himself. His wife had pleaded with him to send someone else after Garcia, but he had not listened. Jose Garcia was a ruthless killer, and had Elfego sent a deputy after him, and the deputy been killed, he would have felt terrible.

There was also the fact that, although his muscles ached, he felt more alive than he had in a long time. One of the reasons he had taken the sheriff's job in Socorro was that he was getting tired of being in the courtroom. He needed more activity—it just hadn't occurred to him that he'd be getting this much!

The bartender had been right about the café and the stew. It had been so good that Elfego had two bowls. When he left the café his belly was full to bursting, and he was straining the buttons on his vest. He had allowed himself to get too portly during his years as an attorney. Maybe a few more forays onto the trail would help him lose some weight.

Whom was he kidding? The only thing that would help him lose weight was to not have that second bowl of stew—or a second helping of *arroz con pollo,* which was his wife's specialty.

He walked down the street, noticing the telephone lines, the occasional automobile going by. How different it had been back when he was nineteen. How different would his life have been if he had not ended up in that *jacal,* if the stubbornness and arrogance of youth had not put him in that position? And how different if the statue of Santa Ana had not been in there with him? All these years later he still felt that the saint had helped him, kept him alive during that whole ordeal.

Perhaps she had been with him all his life since then. How else could he explain his ability to escape all the bad situations he had been in, both inside courtrooms and out on the street? More than once he had been a step away from a prison sentence, or an inch away from death from a bullet or a knife. Thanks to the Lady he was here, in Barnalillo, preparing to capture a deadly killer twenty years younger than he was.

With the help of a sixteen-year-old boy.

As he entered the saloon he saw that it was still pretty slow. The only ones in the saloon at the moment were men with no jobs, the drifters just passing through or, like him, lawmen trying to keep anyone from knowing they were lawmen.

He approached the bartender. "You were right about that stew."

"I know," the man said. "My sister is the cook there. She can cook anything else, as well, and is an excellent housekeeper—"

"I already have a wife."

The bartender spread his hands.

"You cannot blame a brother for trying."

"I wish your sister luck," Elfego said, "but right now I need to speak to young Montoya."

"I saw him, and told him you were looking to hire a guide," the barman said. "He will be here any minute. A beer while you wait?"

"Why not?"

Elfego was halfway through with his beer when the batwing doors swung inward and a youth entered.

"That is Alfredo," the bartender said.

Elfego examined his future guide. To him Montoya looked every inch the sixteen he was supposed to be, but a boy who had been on his own for any period of time could always use a youthful appearance to his advantage. And sixteen could very well be a man, for wasn't he himself only nineteen at the time of the *jacal*? Younger than that, even, when he and Billy the Kid were cowboying together.

Elfego vowed to give the boy the benefit of the doubt.

"Alfredo," the bartender called. "This is Mr. Bonney, the man who is looking for a guide."

The young man approached Elfego with a ready smile and a hearty handshake.

"A pleasure to meet you, Senor Bonney," he said. "Please tell me how I can help you."

"I am told no one knows Sandoval County as you do, Senor Montoya," Elfego said.

The boy blushed and said, "*Sí*, this is true."

"Then I would like to hire you to show me around," Elfego said.

"Are you looking for anything in particular?" the boy asked.

"As a matter of fact," Elfego said, "I am, but why don't we wait until we are on the trail to discuss it?"

"Are you willing to pay?" Montoya asked.

"Handsomely," Elfego said.

"Then when you tell me is up to you, Senor," Montoya said. "When would you like to leave?"

Chapter Forty

"Madre de dios!" Montoya said when Elfego showed him his badge.

They were out on the trail, camping for the first night. From here, Montoya said, they could go in any direction, so Elfego waited until they had a fire going, and a pot of coffee, then took his badge from his pocket and showed it the boy.

"Is this real?" Montoya asked.

"It's real."

"I have done nothing wrong."

"I'm not looking for you, Alfredo," Elfego said, putting the badge away.

"Then who are you searching for, *jefe?*"

"A man named Jose Garcia," Elfego said. "Do you know him?"

214

"I do not," Montoya said, "I swear. What has he done?"

"Killed a man and stole his wife," Elfego said, "and then killed her."

"Dios mio!"

"He cut her into four pieces."

Montoya crossed himself.

"Such a man must be punished."

"Indeed, he must. That is why I am here."

"But you are only one man, *jefe*," Montoya said, "and—forgive me—but you are . . . old."

The word stung, but Elfego Baca maintained his poise. To a boy of sixteen what else would he look?

"That may be," he said, "but I intend to take him back for trial, anyway—or kill him. It will be his choice."

"Senor Jefe," Montoya said, "I wish you luck, truly, but what can I do?"

"I understand that Garcia is working a herd of sheep run by a man named Guittierez."

"See," Montoya said, "I know this man. He hires men who are *muy malo,* very bad men. If you go after Garcia, you will have many other men to go through to get him."

"I will worry about that," Elfego said. "All I want is for you to find the herd and take me to them. I do not know the area, and you do."

"Sí, I know it very well," Montoya said, "and can probably find this herd, but . . ."

Robert J. Randisi

"But what?'

"Excuse me, Senor," Montoya said, "but even if you pay me well I worry that I will not live to spend it."

"Don't worry," Elfego said, "you will live, or my name is not Elfego Baca."

His name had the desired effect on the young man, whose eyes widened. He rocked back on his heels and stared across the fire at Elfego, looking at him with new eyes.

"Truly?" he asked. "You are the hero of the *jacal?*"

"You have heard about that, have you?"

"Oh, *sí,*" Montoya said, "who has not heard of it. It is legendary!"

"Perhaps—"

"But . . . are you truly him?"

"Alfredo," Elfego said, "I don't know what I can do to convince you. I have nothing on me with my name on it. I would not want to be caught and identified until I am ready, eh?"

"*Sí,* this makes sense."

"And I do have the badge of the sheriff of Socorro County, do I not?" Elfego asked.

"*Sí,* you have it."

"And could I have taken it from Elfego Baca?"

Montoya answered without a moment's hesitation.

"No, of course not."

"I am not the Elfego Baca who was in the *ja-*

216

cal," Elfego pointed out. "I am no longer nineteen years old."

Montoya kept staring across the fire, trying to make up his mind whether or not to believe this portly old man.

"Why don't you sleep on it?" Elfego suggested. "In the morning, if you do not want to help me, I will understand."

"*Sí,*" Montoya said, "I will sleep on it, Senor."

"And I will pay you for today, no matter what you decide."

"*Gracias,* Senor."

They wrapped themselves in their blankets and went to sleep. Perhaps in the morning, if the boy decided not to go with him, he could at least point him in the right direction.

Elfego woke first, made coffee and prepared breakfast. He was traveling light, with just coffee and some bacon. He had some beef jerky for when he'd want to make cold camp.

He woke Montoya when breakfast was ready and served it to him with a five-dollar gold piece.

"That's for yesterday," Elfego said. "I wanted to pay you before I heard your decision."

"I will ride with you, Senor Elfego," Montoya said with hesitation.

"Good," Elfego said. "Thank you. What made you decide?"

"Well, you know that you are going after a

217

killer, and that he will be with many other bad men."

"Yes, I do."

"And you still intend to go after him."

"That's right."

Montoya shrugged.

"Who else but the hero of the *jacal* would do such a crazy thing?"

Elfego smiled at the boy. Who else, indeed?

Chapter Forty-one

On the second night out Elfego Baca began to burn cork, which he had purchased before leaving Bernalillo.

"What is that for?" Montoya asked.

"It's for a plan I have," Elfego said. "I will need a disguise if we are going into the shepherds' camp."

"A disguise? I thought you didn't know anyone in their camp."

"Well, since I don't know who is in the camp, I can't be sure I don't know any of them," Elfego said. "But I do know Garcia, and he knows me. So I need a disguise."

"What kind of disguise?"

Elfego took Montoya's hand, picked up a piece

of cork, and made a black line across the boy's hand.

"This kind."

Montoya looked at his hand in the light from the fire.

"It's black."

"Yes, it is," Elfego said, "and so will I be when I smear it all over myself."

"So . . . you will be going into the camp as a *negro*?"

"Exactly," Elfego said, "but not as any negro . . . as your groom."

"Ah," Montoya said. "Not only will no one recognize you, they probably will not even look at you."

"Correct. Oh, and there's something I didn't ask you before, Alfredo," Elfego said.

"What is that, *jefe*?"

"Do you know any of the men in the camp?"

"I am not sure," the young man said. "I am known to everyone in town—almost in the whole county."

"So then there's a good chance some of them will know you."

"I guess . . ."

"That's good," Elfego said, "that's very good, Alfredo. Now, you must help me with this."

"With the . . . blackness?"

"Yes," Elfego said, taking off his shirt. "There are places on my body I cannot reach myself."

"On your . . . body?" Montoya asked, horrified. "You want me to . . . to put the black on you?"

"Just certain places," Elfego said.

"Senor, I cannot—"

"I will pay you extra."

"Well . . ."

"Besides," Elfego said, "we are only going to black my body in places that might be seen."

Montoya eyed Elfego's belly and said, "That is good, senor. For a minute I did not think we would have enough."

Chapter Forty-two

Elfego slept with the blackface on, to see if it stayed in place. For the most part it did, but he decided not to patch where it had come off. He wanted to see how it stayed on while they were riding in the heat.

"Won't it wash off when you sweat?"

"We'll see, won't we?"

They broke camp and rode off, looking for all the world like a Mexican boy with a black groom following behind him.

It took six long days for Montoya to find the shepherds. Several times he apologized to Elfego for getting them lost, but the lawman had faith in the boy and said so. He never scolded or berated him, and on the sixth say they came within sight of the fires from the shepherds' camp.

They camped that night without a fire, dining on beef jerky for both supper and breakfast. In the morning they worked on Elfego's body with the black burnt cork they had left, blackening his skin everyplace it might peek out from his clothes.

When they were done, they mounted up and rode for the shepherds' camp.

It was farther away then they thought, and they didn't get to the camp until around suppertime.

They took the time to scout around to make sure they knew how many men they were dealing with. Also, Elfego had to decide if he should send Montoya in alone first, or if he should go along with him.

He decided that it wouldn't do any good to send the boy in alone. He didn't know what Garcia looked like. Also, Elfego was itching to get this thing over with. And, if he rode in with the boy he would not draw that much attention, since he was just a "negro" as far as they were concerned. If Montoya rode in first and he came after, they might pay more attention to him. Elfego did not know how his blackface would stand up to close scrutiny.

He decided they would ride in together.

"I need a gun," the boy said when they were ready.

"What for?" They had not discussed this before.

"So I can help you."

"Do you usually carry a gun?"

"No."

"If we ride in there and some of the men know you, won't they think it odd that you have a gun?"

"But . . . I want to help."

"Can you even shoot, Alfredo?"

"I can pull the trigger."

"That doesn't do anybody any good," Elfego said. "You might even shoot me. No, you don't need a gun. Leave all the shooting to me."

"I am frightened, Elfego," Montoya said.

"Don't be," Elfego said. "I will handle everything. All you have to do is sit back and watch."

"What if something goes wrong?" Montoya asked. "They will know I brought you. They will kill me."

"I am not going to let anyone kill you, Alfredo."

Montoya was breathing hard. He turned and walked away from his horse. This was not a good time for the boy to lose his nerve. Elfego could not ride in there alone.

He walked over to the boy, put his hand on his shoulder.

"If you do not want to ride into that camp, I will not force you," he said. "But I have to, and without you I stand a good chance of getting killed."

"I am sorry—"

"Together," Elfego said, "we have a good chance of coming out alive, and with Garcia."

Montoya turned and looked at him.

"Is that the truth?"

"Yes."

"But . . . they are many."

"There were eighty at the *jacal*," Elfego said, "and yet here I am, no?"

"*Si.*"

"Come," Elfego said, "be brave and I will keep both of us alive—or I am not Elfego Baca."

He hated to brag, but the boy needed it from him. He had to seem so confident that the boy would forget any fear of being hurt or killed.

"Are you ready, Alfredo?" Elfego asked.

He gave the young man credit. Montoya took a long, deep breath, then smiled and said, "I am ready, *jefe.*"

Chapter Forty-three

Dusk was approaching as Alfredo Montoya and his "groom" rode to the edge of the arroyo where the shepherds had their camp. They could hear the sheep calling out to each other as they settled in for the night. Some of the herders were mounted, others were gathered around the fire. They all turned to look at the two approaching riders with suspicion, hands hovering around their holsters.

"Call out to them," Elfego said, "just in case there are some who know you."

"*Amigos,*" Montoya shouted, "it is me, Alfredo Montoya."

As luck would have it, several of the men knew who Montoya was.

"Hey, Alfredo!" one of them called out.

Their postures relaxed, and to Elfego's relief their hands fell away from their guns.

"Come in, Alfredo," another called. "You're just in time to eat with us."

As Montoya and Elfego began to ride into camp, the men suddenly noticed the second man. Once again their hands moved toward their guns.

"Who is that with you, Alfredo?" one asked.

"That is my groom," Montoya shouted.

Several of the men shifted position so they could see Elfego, but they did not move closer to examine him. Immediately, they took him at face value.

"*Negros.*" someone shouted, and they began to laugh.

The men relaxed, and so, too, did Montoya. However, Elfego was looking around the camp carefully, trying to spot Jose Garcia. Suddenly, he spotted him standing in the background, near his horse. Both of his hands were busy working on a lariat. He wasn't wearing his gun, but the holster was hanging from his saddle and was only inches from his hands.

Elfego dismounted first and hurried to hold Montoya's stirrup for him as the boy stepped down. He was careful to keep his blackened face turned away so that no one could get a very good look at him. He could feel his sweat dripping down his neck, and he had no idea how much of the cork might be going with it. He especially did not want Garcia to get a good look at him until he was ready to make his move.

Elfego moved along behind Montoya, watching Garcia like a hawk. At the first opportunity he was going to produce both his guns, and he hoped that no one else would panic before he was able to identify himself. He was hoping that his name alone would give them pause and keep them from helping Garcia.

The men on horseback drifted away, and they were left with three men around the fire and Garcia in the background. Elfego awaited his chance, happy that the others had moved away. Finally, Garcia seemed to relax, and just for a moment turned his head away. When he turned back he was covered by Elfego Baca's guns.

"Hands up! Now, Garcia!" Elfego shouted.

Instantly, Garcia recognized the voice and realized who the "negro" was.

"Elfego Baca," he said.

"Wha—" one of the men around the fire said, but young Montoya had taken the initiative. He grabbed Elfego's rifle from his saddle and covered the men around the fire.

"Hands up!" he shouted, his voice almost squeaking with nervousness, but the three stuck their hands in the air immediately. The only thing worse than having a gun pointed at you by a professional is having one pointed at you by a nervous amateur.

"Move toward the fire," Elfego ordered Garcia, who moved over to join the other three.

"Get their guns, Alfredo," Elfego instructed.

Alfredo did as he was told, disarming all three men, who looked more gunmen than shepherds. Elfego then took his own lariat and used it to pin Garcia's hands to his side. All the while he was suffering the hard looks of the other three. He felt he had to say something to keep them from following when they left.

"Jose Garcia is a killer," he said aloud. "He shot a man, took his wife, and then cut her into four pieces when he was done with her. We are taking him back to Socorro to stand trial." He took his badge out and showed it to them. "I am the law. If any of you try to rescue him, I will be justified in killing you. Remain here and do not follow. Do you understand me?"

All three men nodded.

Elfego and Alfredo took turns covering the men while they put Garcia on his horse. Elfego tied the other end of his lariat to his saddle. Then he had Alfredo mount, and covered him while he mounted.

They rode out with Alfredo in the front, Garcia between them, and Elfego Baca taking up the rear. Looking back, he saw that the three men had put their hands down, but none had reached for their guns or made a move toward their horses.

"Are they following?" Alfredo asked, afraid to look.

"They are not, Alfredo," Elfego said.

He could hear the boy's sigh of relief.

"You did very well back there, Alfredo," Elfego said. "You will make a fine lawman someday."

Alfredo did not look back, but Elfego could see him sit up straighter in his saddle, his back stiff with pride.

Chapter Forty-four

Because they had traveled in circles at times and the shepherds had been moving, it had taken six days for Montoya to find the camp. Now that they were traveling in a straight line and knew where they were going, it took only eight hours to ride to Thornton, a small town on the Santa Fe railroad line.

The three men attracted a lot of attention when they rode in, especially with one tied up the way he was, obviously a prisoner. They halted their procession in front of the local jail, and Elfego dismounted.

"Wait out here and keep an eye on him," he told Montoya. "I'm going to talk to the sheriff."

He walked into the office and saw a young

man wearing a deputy's badge seated behind the desk.

The deputy was shocked at the sight of Elfego Baca, who was still wearing much of his black cork disguise.

"Who the hell—"

Elfego showed him his Socorro County sheriff's badge. "I am Sheriff Elfego Baca. I have a prisoner outside and want to use your jail for a little while."

"Sheriff—"

"Where's your sheriff?"

"Elfego Baca?" the young man repeated.

"That's right," Elfego said. "I am in disguise and haven't had time to wash it off. Where is the sheriff?"

"Sheriff's office is in the county seat," the man said. "I'm Deputy Jack Simmons—"

"Deputy," Elfego said, losing patience, "I need your jail."

"Ain't got one," the man said.

"What?"

"No jail cells here, uh, Sheriff . . . Baca?" The young man was still trying to look past the black cork face.

Elfego looked around the small office and spotted a pitcher and basin with a rag next to them.

"Maybe this will help," he said. He walked over, wet the rag, and started wiping cork from his face. By the time he was done he was recognizable as a white man, but hardly as himself.

"Look past the black face, boy," he said, scolding the deputy. "I have a prisoner outside. Jose Garcia."

"The killer?"

"Now you're getting it," Elfego said. "I need someplace to keep him until the next train to Albuquerque pulls in."

"Well, your best bet is to take him to the train station," the young man said. "The depot building is the newest one in town, and the sturdiest."

"The depot?"

"Yes, sir."

What the hell, Elfego thought. At least they would be there when the train pulled in.

He started for the door, then stopped and looked at the deputy.

"Keep this under your hat, boy," he said. "I don't need everybody in your town knowing I have Jose Garcia with me. *Comprende?*"

"Yes, sir, I understand real good."

Elfego nodded and left the office. No sooner was he gone than the deputy grabbed his hat, went out the back door, and started spreading the word that the killer Jose Garcia was in town.

"Where are we going?" Alfredo Montoya asked as Elfego mounted his horse.

"The train depot," he said. "This town has no jail."

Elfego took the lead and kept Garcia between them by having Montoya bring up the rear.

When they reached the depot, he told Montoya to dismount and then they took Garcia off his horse. They had attracted a crowd of curious onlookers by this time.

They went into the depot, and Elfego stuck Garcia on a wooden bench.

"Watch him," he told Montoya, who was still holding Elfego's rifle.

Elfego approached the ticket agent. "When is the next train to Albuquerque?"

"Four hours," the man answered.

"Elfego!" Montoya called. "Look outside."

Elfego moved to the window. A mob had gathered around the building, and he guessed by the looks on their faces that they knew who was inside.

"Give us Garcia!" someone shouted.

"Bring the killer out!"

"Hang him!"

"*Madre de dios!*" Elfego whispered.

He produced one gun and, waving it aimlessly, asked the ticket agent, "When is the next train to anywhere?"

Chapter Forty-five

The next train was scheduled to arrive in fifteen minutes, going in the opposite direction of Albuquerque.

Elfego could hear the crowd at the door, but as yet no one had the courage to try to open it and come in.

The lawman moved to the door and shouted, "What do you want?" even though he knew the answer.

"We want Jose Garcia!" a voice called back.

"We want the killer of women!" another called.

"*Asesino!*"

Garcia looked at Elfego, wide-eyed with fear. "You can't let them have me!"

"Don't worry," Alfredo said. "He is Elfego

235

Baca, the hero of the *jacal*. He can hold them off."

Elfego didn't know how many men were outside the building, but he wasn't so sure he could hold them off, especially not without *Mi Senora Santa Ana*. Idly, he took a moment to wonder where that statue was right then.

The door shuddered as the crowd surged and the men in front were pressed against it.

"They'll break through!" the ticket clerk said, ducking down behind his counter.

"Alfredo," Elfego said, "stay by Garcia."

"What are you going to do?"

"I'm going to try to convince them they're making a mistake," Elfego said.

"Can you hold them off?" Garcia asked.

"I don't know," Elfego said.

"It is only fifteen minutes," Alfredo Montoya said with confidence. "You can do it."

"We will see," Elfego said. He drew his guns and walked to the door. "Open it, Alfredo, and then close it quickly behind me."

"*Sí*, 'Fego," Alfredo said. "Good luck."

"Thank you," Elfego said. "I'll need it."

He nodded, and Alfredo threw the door open.

At the sudden appearance of Elfego Baca in the doorway the crowd, which had been surging forward, fell back. It helped that Elfego still wore much of the cork and presented a rather frightening visage as he stood there, pistols in hand.

The crowd grew quiet.

"Garcia is my prisoner," Elfego announced. "I am taking him out of here on the next train."

"Hang the murderer here!" someone shouted.

"We want Garcia!"

The voices came from the back of the crowd, where the people were calling for those in front to act.

"Go on. Take him."

"Push him out of the way."

The men in front were not quite as brave as those in the back, however.

"You'd better give him to us," one of the men in front said. "He deserves to die."

"He is not worth getting hurt for." someone said.

"That may be, but you will have to take him from me," Elfego said, "and that means that some of you will die."

He let those words hang in the air for a few moments before continuing.

"Which of you are ready to sacrifice yourselves so that the others may enjoy a lynching?"

The crowd started to fidget, looking around at each other, seeking the ones who would make the sacrifice.

"Who are you?" someone asked.

Elfego squared his shoulders and hoped that his name would have the desired effect.

"I," he said, "am Elfego Baca."

There was a gasp from the crowd. Several people whispered his name, and he heard someone say the word . . . *jacal*. He allowed his name to hang in the air for a few moments, let them digest it, taste it.

"Think about it," Elfego said. "Make your choice . . . but make it wisely."

He kicked at the door with his heel, and Alfredo opened it. Elfego backed inside and slammed it shut.

"Did that work?" Alfredo asked.

"It gave them something to think about," Elfego said, holstering his weapons. "How long they will think, though, I don't know."

Chapter Forty-six

Watching the clock, Elfego wondered what would come first, the train or the mob's courage. He could hear them talking among themselves out there, arguing the pros and cons of rushing Elfego Baca. That's why Elfego hoped that the Miracle of the Jacal was fresh in everyone's mind.

Garcia sat on his bench with his hands tied behind him, sweating profusely.

Alfredo Montoya seemed supremely confident. He had seen Elfego Baca stand up to the crowd once, and he was certain that he would be able to do it again.

The clerk remained behind his counter, looking worried, prepared to drop to the floor at a moment's notice.

"There is no other way to get to the train?" Elfego asked him.

"No, sir," the clerk said. "You got to walk out that door and walk along the platform."

"They'll kill me," Garcia said. "You cannot take me out there, Elfego."

"You should have thought of that before you decided to cut that woman into four parts, Jose. Did she plead, also?"

Garcia did not answer.

Elfego went to the window and looked out. The crowd had not grown smaller. If anything, it had swelled in size. That damned deputy must have spread the word far and wide.

Five minutes more, that was all he asked. . . .

The sound of the train whistle broke the silence that had been lingering for four minutes. There was not a sound inside or out. All Elfego thought he could hear was the collective breathing of the mob.

"Here she comes," the clerk said.

"Get him up," Elfego said to Alfredo. "You are going to walk him to the train."

"W-what are you going to do?" Alfredo asked.

"I'm going to cover you." Elfego drew both his guns.

"Two guns against that mob?" Garcia demanded.

"I will go out first," Elfego said. "Come out when I kick the door. All right?"

"*Sí.* 'Fego."

"You can do this," Elfego said.

Alfredo gave him a brave smile. "We can do it."

"Yes," Elfego said, and went outside.

Once again the crowd moved back as Elfego Baca appeared in the doorway with his guns out.

"I am sure you can all hear the train approaching," he said loudly. "We are getting on that train with Jose Garcia."

"Over our dead bodies," someone shouted, but it was a voice way in the back and the speaker could not be recognized.

"You are very brave," Elfego said derisively. "All of you listen. I will kill any man who tries to stop us from getting on that train. That is a solemn promise."

The crowd buzzed, but they knew who he was now and they were impressed.

"Stay back!" he commanded, and kicked the door behind him.

The door opened and Alfredo came out, bringing Garcia behind him. Elfego allowed the boy and the desperado to go ahead of him to the train platform and then he brought up the rear, keeping the mob covered with both of his guns.

He knew that if someone wanted to take a shot at Garcia now there was little he could do about it. All it took was one brave man with a rifle who could hit a man from a distance. Elfego probably would not even know where the shot came from.

Alfredo moved at a crab's pace, apparently afraid that sudden moves might spur the crowd on.

"Let's go a little faster, Alfredo," Elfego said, and the boy quickened his pace.

Suddenly, they were on the platform and the train was not there yet. They were out in the open, easy targets, but still the crowd stayed back, although they were starting to get loud again.

"Come on, let's get 'em!" someone in the back shouted.

"Don't let them get away."

Always, Elfego thought, the brave ones are in the back.

Suddenly, the train appeared. It pulled alongside the platform and came to a halt, and a conductor stepped down. He saw the crowd, saw the men awaiting him on the platform.

"I'm taking a prisoner aboard your train," Elfego said, showing the man the badge.

"Anyone can board the train," the conductor said, apparently unconcerned.

"Go, Alfredo," Elfego said.

The young man boarded the train, and Elfego pushed Garcia up to join him. The legendary lawman turned one more time to look at the mob and show them his guns before boarding. Alfredo had taken Garcia inside the train, but Elfego remained outside lest someone get brave and try to board after them.

"No one else?" the conductor asked.

"Let's get moving, Conductor," Elfego said.

The conductor turned to look at Elfego, apparently prepared to say something, but something in Elfego's eyes—or his corked face—changed his mind.

"Board!" he shouted, and climbed onto the train himself.

He waved down the platform to someone in the engine, who waved back. Slowly, the train began to move. Elfego remained where he was, between cars. He doubted that any of the crowd would have the courage to try to board the train while it was still moving, but better to be safe than sorry.

As he passed the main bulk of the crowd, someone shouted something and he brought his guns up before he realized what had been said.

It was: "*Adiós*, Elfego. Good luck."

Apparently, once the prisoner was beyond their reach the crowd had turned.

Elfego leaned out and waved once, then holstered his guns and joined Alfredo Montoya and Jose Garcia inside the train.

Interlude

The reporter paused in his writing for a moment and looked across the table at Elfego Baca.

"So once again you held off a mob," he said. "That seems to have been a specialty of yours."

"A mob is only as brave as its bravest member," Elfego said, "but that member also has to be in the front, not shouting from the back."

"But . . . I don't understand how you can stand before a mob with only two guns."

"It is simple," Elfego said. "Any mob knows that it will lose a few members if it makes a move toward the man with the gun."

"And?"

"And no one wants to be that person," Elfego said. "No one wants to be the one who gets shot so that the others can have their way. What good is a lynching if you can't be there to see it?"

"When you explain it like that it sounds very simple," the reporter said. "Still, I don't think I could ever face down a mob."

"It's not your job," Elfego Baca said. "It was mine."

The reporter was impressed with the fact that Elfego Baca did not seem to realize how brave a man he had been throughout his life.

"Actually," Elfego said, thoughtfully, "you don't even necessarily need a gun to face down a larger group—like twelve."

"Like a jury," the reporter said, when hearing the number.

"Exactly."

"What?"

"Once," Elfego said, "I was on trial for shooting a man—"

"That seems to have happened quite often," the reporter commented.

"Well," Elfego said, very deliberately, "this was one of those times. . . ."

"I was on trial for killing a man, and there were quite a few witnesses who said I did it in cold blood. My defense attorney, George Armijo, thought we were in a bad way.

" 'I don't know how to get you out of this one, 'Fego,' he said to me. 'The only witness I have for you is . . . you.'

" 'Just keep the trial going for two weeks, George,' I told him.

" 'But . . . how—'

" 'It doesn't matter how,' I told him, 'just keep it going. Stall, any way you can. Just don't let it go to the jury for two more weeks.'

"From that day on I turned my chair to face the jury and, each day, I chose a different juror to stare at. This was just a few years ago, so my countenance was not that of a young man, but an older one. I have these bushy eyebrows, you see, but what some people seem to think is an elderly gleam in my eye can easily be turned cold.'

"Meanwhile, George was doing his best to drag the trial out, trying the patience of the judge as he did so. There were so many witnesses for the prosecution that all he had to do was hang on to each one as long as possible.

"He'd 'Ho,' and 'Hum,' and the judge would demand, 'Get on with the questions, Counselor!'

"But George was steadfast, as he was my friend as well as my lawyer. He would ask the witness, 'How old are you?' and 'How many children do you have?' and 'How old are they?' until the prosecutor objected and the judge sustained the objection.

"With one witness he asked, 'Has anyone in your family ever had smallpox?' and both the prosecutor and the judge exploded. 'Get on with the shooting and leave smallpox alone,' the judge instructed in no uncertain terms.

"Meanwhile, I stared and stared at the jurors. Some for half a day, some for as much as two days in a row.

"In the end it went to the jury, and the judge just about ordered them to come back and find me guilty. They were out ten minutes, came back, and pronounced me not guilty . . ."

"You intimidated an entire jury just by glaring at them?" the reporter asked, amazed.

"Well, not just me," Elfego replied modestly. "You see, George put my brother Francisco on the stand. He testified that he had seen me hit a jackrabbit with my pistol at fifty feet while at a full gallop on a horse."

"And that helped?"

"What helped was that everyone in town knew that Francisco could do that at *one hundred* feet. My brother also testified as how he would be hard pressed to bear any good feeling toward someone who did me harm. In saying that he turned his head and stared directly at the jury."

"So it was you and your brother who intimidated them."

"Well," Elfego said, "that and undoubtedly the fact that I was not guilty."

"But you did shoot the man?"

"Oh, yes, I shot him," Elfego said, "but he had it coming."

The reporter raised his eyebrows, shook his head, and finished writing in his notebook.

"Now," Elfego said, "on to that story of when I was the chief of a gambling hall police force. That was at the Tivoli, in El Paso. It was 1921. . . ."

Four
The Tivoli . . .
The Bouncer and the
Songbird . . .
. . . Numero Ocho . . .

Chapter Forty-seven

The Tivoli was a wonderful gambling establishment in El Paso. Four men named Senors Revilla, Rebia, Lopez, and Asteca paid about $84,000 a month American money for the gambling concession there. It was a huge investment, but well worth it, as the Tivoli was *the* place to gamble in El Paso. Accordingly, the four gentlemen decided they needed the best of the best to head their security force, and so they hired the legendary Elfego Baca to be the chief of their private gambling police force. Elfego was taking down $750 a month for this job, and for the most part he simply allowed his four bosses to let it be known far and wide that Elfego Baca, the hero of the jacal, was head of security.

Elfego's job was rather simple. He oversaw a

fourteen-man force that made sure everything went smoothly inside the Tivoli. Elfego's job began every morning at 11:00 A.M., when he oversaw the paying of all the establishment's employees. The payroll of the police, the dealers, and the other workers in the place came to $4,500 a month.

Elfego also watched over all the dealers, making sure that they ran their tables cleanly, and did not skim or take any graft for themselves. In addition, he and his fourteen-man force were prepared for any kind of a raid attempt on the Tivoli.

The Tivoli had a dual lighting system, whereby if someone tried to cut the power in order to raid the place, a second lighting system automatically came on in an instant. And, of course, Elfego and his men were ready to use their guns at a moment's notice to fend off would-be raiders. When Elfego left his employment there, he left behind a perfect record—not one successful raid under his watch.

During his time at the Tivoli Elfego made the acquaintance of two people whose fame stemmed from two diametrically opposed walks of life, and stirred two very different emotions inside the legendary lawman.

During the course of one afternoon's gambling Elfego noticed a ruckus at one of the roulette tables. The Tivoli expected their customers to gamble in such a way as to avoid any dramatic revelry. In truth regulars had learned that, no matter what the windfall, they were to celebrate it as quietly as possible.

However, the lady playing at the roulette table was not a regular, and was ignorant of this particular Tivoli rule. It fell to Elfego Baca to educate her.

He approached the table as the lady's number came up again, for the second time in a row. She and her party made such a fuss that nearby faro and blackjack dealers looked over with distaste.

Elfego approached the party, watching before he made his way to the front to stand next to the lady who was the cause of the celebration.

They turned their heads at the same time, looked at each other, and this is what they saw: he, a lovely face, pale skin, full lips, as pretty a lady as he had ever seen on either side of the border; she, a portly, mustachioed, rather rough-looking gent of fifty-five or so, smiling broadly at her in a very disarming way.

"Hello!" she said tentatively, for she did not know who he was or why he was standing next to her, smiling at her.

"Please, go right ahead and gamble," he said. "I'm the chief of security here, just a glorified bouncer, really, but I'll have to ask you to keep your party a little quieter."

"That seems fair," she said. "I'm afraid I'm the one who is causing the ruckus, though. This is all so new to me." She stuck her hand out and said, "I'm Mary Garden."

"I'm Elfego Baca," he said, shaking her hand.

It appeared that each was completely ignorant as to who the other was. Elfego's knowledge of the theater was such that he had no idea he was in the presence of one of the premier songbirds in the country. She, on the other hand, had no idea of the legend of the man whose hand she was shaking.

Around them, people who knew of them both found the tableau very amusing: the bouncer and the songbird.

It was some time later, after they got to know each other, that the two became more informed as to who the other was. While not terribly impressed, they nevertheless found that they enjoyed each other's company.

Elfego took Mary Garden out the next day and showed her El Paso and Juarez, and she in turn took him back to the hotel with her and gave him tickets for her show.

Elfego took Francisquita to hear Mary Garden sing, and while he didn't like it very much in the theater he applauded enthusiastically when she was finished.

On the way home his wife asked, "Did you like that?"

"She has a lovely voice," he replied, "but I

don't think I like the theater experience very much. Much too noisy for me."

"Nosier than the Tivoli?" she asked.

"Oh, much," he said. "I enjoy the Mexican string bands much more."

Francisquita smiled, shook her head at her husband's disregard for the higher arts, and held tightly to his arm.

Chapter Forty-eight

Probably the main reason Elfego Baca was hired to head security at the Tivoli was a man called Numero Ocho, who was the head of the Juarez underworld. Ocho was a thorn in the sides of the four men who ran gambling at the Tivoli, but, to their credit, none of the four men hid this fact from Elfego Baca. . . .

When Elfego was first interviewed by the four, Revilla, Rebia, Lopez, and Asteca—or perhaps it was he who was interviewing them—he was surprised to find all of them waiting when he entered the Tivoli's management office. They were dressed similarly, in dark suits and ties, and seemed to all be between the ages of forty-five and fifty-five. Indeed, they seemed physically interchangeable.

They shook hands all around, making introductions, and Elfego asked, "Who does the hiring?"

"We all do," Revilla responded.

Elfego soon realized that he would never know which of the four would respond to a direct question or statement. They were apparently not only interchangeable physically, but in every other way, as well. He was impressed by the way they operated together.

"Allow us to explain the job as we see it," Lopez said, and went on to describe what Elfego's duties would be.

"Seems straightforward enough," Elfego said. "What would the pay be?"

Rebia told him about the $750 a week. "In addition, we expect you to supervise payday each week, and you can take twenty-five dollars more off the top each time."

"Is that all of it?" Elfego asked.

The four men exchanged glances all the way around.

"Why do you ask?" Asteca responded.

"The job seems simple enough," Elfego said. "I think you could get someone other than me to do it a lot cheaper."

"We don't want cheap," Rebia said.

"We want good," Revilla added.

"We want the best," Lopez put in.

"And then," Asteca said, "there is the matter of Numero Ocho."

"Ah," Elfego said, folding his hands over his belly. "Now we get to it."

"Have you heard of Numero Ocho?" Rebia asked.

"Of course I have," Elfego said. "He runs all illegal activities in Juarez, and occasionally crosses the International Bridge."

"To give us hell," Lopez said.

"So part of my job," Elfego said, "will be to keep you and your business safe from Numero Ocho and his gang."

For the first time the four men seemed unsure as to who should answer the question.

Finally, it was Revilla who said, "Yes, that's exactly it."

"How many men do I have working under me?"

"Fourteen," Rebia said, "and they are yours to do with as you wish. Hire, fire, whatever you like."

Elfego thought about asking who the men were and where they were from, but he decided to simply meet and evaluate them himself.

"All right," Elfego said. "I will take the job."

All four men perked up, as if they thought that mentioning Numero Ocho was going to be a deal breaker.

"When can you start?" Lopez asked.

"Tomorrow morning," Elfego said. "I will take tonight to simply walk around and look the operation over. In the morning, I would like to meet all of my men."

"I will arrange that," Asteca said.

"I will need a small advance on my salary," Elfego said.

They were prepared for that. Revilla took a brown envelope from a desk drawer and passed it over to Elfego. It was thick with U.S. greenbacks.

"A week's salary," Revilla said. "Consider it a bonus."

Elfego smiled, put the envelope in his pocket, and said, "I like the way you do business . . . so far."

The men all stood and shook hands again.

"Tell me," Elfego asked, before leaving the office, "who do I report to?"

"All of us," Revilla said.

Elfego frowned.

"Is that a problem?" Rebia asked.

"I would prefer to report to one man, if that is possible," Elfego said. "I believe it would make my job easier. If you need time to talk it over and decide who that will be—"

"You can report to me," Rebia said.

He was neither the youngest of the four, nor the oldest. He seemed to be right in the middle, which suited Elfego somehow.

"Very well," Elfego said. "You and I can talk

again after I have looked the place over and met all the men."

"Agreed," Rebia said.

Elfego left, leaving the four very satisfied with the meeting. For the most part, Elfego was satisfied too. He knew the reputation of the Tivoli and he knew the reputation of Numero Ocho. He would certainly have a meeting with the gang leader, but first he would take the time to learn a little about the men under him, and a lot about the men above him.

After all these years, he was nothing if not thorough.

Chapter Forty-nine

Elfego Baca entered the room and took an objective look at his private police force of fourteen men. They seemed to range in age from twenty to fifty. As he entered he heard their voices, previously raised in conversation, go quiet. They were studying him as closely as he was them. What they knew of Elfego Baca and what they saw probably didn't quite mix. Over time, they'd get to know him, and realize that you can't judge a man by the way he looks. If he was going to do that he would have fired half of them on the spot.

He had looked over the gambling establishment the day before, and had been impressed. He had seen one dealer already who was stealing, but he decided to leave him for another time. The man looked to be taking only a small amount of money from time to time.

Today, he was going to get to know these men. They were all sitting in what was a common room, where they would keep their clothes and belongings. Off to one side was an office that had been set up for him.

"I am Elfego Baca," he said to the assembled. "As of today, I am your boss. I want to see each of you in my office, one at a time. You decide the order, but I'll start with you." He pointed to a man who was short and stocky and looked to be about fifty years old. "What's your name?"

"Alphonso," the man said.

"You'll come inside with me now," Elfego said. To the rest he said, "I'll try not to take too long with each of you. When we're finished you can go right to work."

"Some of us have the day off," a man said. He appeared to be the youngest and his tone of voice and demeanor were clearly challenging.

"Is that a fact?" Elfego asked. "What's your name?"

"Raphael."

"Raphael what?"

"Salvador."

"Well, Raphael," Elfego asked, "do you have today off?"

"I was supposed to," the boy said belligerently.

"I see," Elfego said. "I tell you what. You come in to see me last."

"What? Last?" Raphael complained. "But I'll be here all day!"

"You should have thought of that before you opened your mouth," the new chief of security said. "Alphonso, follow me."

"*Sí jefe,*" the man said.

Speaking to the men one at a time, Elfego discovered that he had five ex-policemen, three ex-soldiers, an ex-Pinkerton detective, and four other men with no law enforcement experience, but varied experience when it came to jobs.

And then there was the kid, Raphael.

When it was finally his turn to come into the room, he did so with his shoulders slumped and his chin stuck out.

"What did you do before this job, Raphael?"

"I worked in a livery stable."

"Was that your first job?"

"Yes."

"So this is your second?"

"Yes."

"How long have you been here?"

"Three months."

"You have a bad attitude."

"How do you know?" Raphael asked. "You only just got here."

"It's very obvious."

"You gonna fire me?"

"I don't know," Elfego said, "should I?"

"I don't know," Raphael said. Then, grudgingly, he added, "I like this job."

"But?"

"But . . . I don't think they should have hired you."

"Why not?"

"You're . . . old," Raphael said. "I mean, I know who you're supposed to be . . . who you were . . . but now . . ."

"You think I'm too old to still be Elfego Baca?"

"You have a reputation," the boy said.

"And you think that's what they hired me for?" Elfego said. "My reputation?"

The boy didn't answer.

"A reputation is not going to keep Numero Ocho out of the Tivoli, Raphael."

"You'll never keep Numero Ocho out," the boy said. "Never." His admiration for the gangster was evident. Elfego had been wondering if one or more of the men might not actually be working for Numero Ocho. Now he wondered about Raphael.

"All right, Raphael," Elfego said.

"You gonna fire me?"

"Not right now," Elfego said, "but we'll see. Go, enjoy the rest of your day off."

As the boy left the office, Elfego sat back in his chair. He was going to keep the nine men who had experience and replace the other four. He hadn't decided what he was going to do about Raphael, though. That would come later.

Chapter Fifty

Elfego spent the next few weeks getting his private police force in order. He interviewed new men, and with each one he hired he fired one of the inexperienced ones. Finally, he had himself a police force of thirteen experienced men—and Raphael.

Elfego watched Raphael when he worked. For some reason he liked the boy, but it wasn't until he was telling Francisquita about him one night that he found out why.

"Why, 'Fego, you silly man," she said across the supper table.

"What?"

"He reminds you of yourself when you were that age," she said. "He's brash, arrogant, but has some natural ability, *verdad?*"

"Yes," Elfego said finally, "it is true, my love. But I'm worried."

"About what?"

"He seems to have this . . . hero worship for Numero Ocho."

"What a ridiculous name for a man," she commented. "Naming himself after a number."

"Whatever his name is, the boy admires him."

"And he thinks you're old."

"Yes."

His wife leaned across the table, covered one of his hands with hers, and said, "You will change his mind, my love."

Elfego lifted his wife's hand to his lips and kissed it.

Numero Ocho knew about the hiring of Elfego Baca even before Elfego came to town. He had learned it from the man he had planted inside the Tivoli.

In a cantina in Juarez Numero Ocho spoke with the two men he trusted most in his gang, Esteban and Carlos.

"*Jefe,*" Carlos said, "this Elfego Baca, he has been working at the Tivoli for weeks now and still we have not seen him. Perhaps he does not intend to come after you?"

"Oh, he will," Numero Ocho said. "He has to. That is what he was hired to do. Also, his own arrogance will force him to."

"Arrogance?" Esteban asked.

"He is Elfego Baca, is he not?" Numero Ocho asked.

"But . . . he is an old Elfego Baca," Esteban said. "How can he be a match for you?"

"These old legends," Numero Ocho said, "they never realize that they are old. They think they can do the same things at fifty that they did when they were twenty. He will learn," the gang leader said with a smile, "and I will enjoy teaching him."

When he had been at the Tivoli for a month, Elfego reported to Rebia that he had his force the way he wanted it.

"I still have fourteen men, but now I have the fourteen men I want," he said.

"That's good," Rebia said. "I noticed that you kept that inexperienced young man . . . Raphael?"

"Yes, I did."

"Why?"

"Several reasons," Elfego said. "One, he seems to idolize Numero Ocho."

"That is a reason to keep him?"

"Not yet," Elfego said. "Two, he reminds me of me when I was that age."

"Ah," Rebia said, "that is the reason."

"No," Elfego said. "Three, I believe he is working for Numero Ocho."

"He's a spy?" Rebia asked.

"Exactly."

"And that is the reason you kept him on?"

"Yes."

"I don't understand."

"Trust me," Elfego said. "It will all come out well in the end."

Rebia did trust Elfego, as did his three partners. Three days into the job, Elfego had told Rebia that he'd found a dealer cheating. The man was fired. At that point Elfego Baca had saved them money, already earning his keep.

Also, once the word got out that he worked there people came to see the legendary hero of the *jacal*. While they were there, they stayed and gambled.

Elfego was worth what they were paying him and more, but there was still the matter of Numero Ocho.

"I can't understand it," Rebia said. "He's never left us alone for this long."

"He's waiting," Elfego said.

"For what?"

"To see if I come after him."

"And will you?"

"Maybe," Elfego said, "but not for a while. Let him wait and think about it."

"You think that's wise?"

"An impatient gangster," Elfego Baca said to Rebia, "is a careless gangster."

Chapter Fifty-one

Elfego Baca and Numero Ocho began playing mind games with each other over the next few weeks. Elfego started talking—especially around Raphael—about how he had little or no respect for a man who went around calling himself by a number rather than a name.

By the same token, Numero Ocho told anyone who would listen what he would do to Elfego Baca if they ever came face-to-face.

Elfego had taken to keeping Raphael with him when he did his rounds. Over the course of his first month he had managed to sniff out even the hint of a ruckus and put it down before it got out of hand. They were not all as easy as Mary Garden, and in some cases Elfego had to show something he didn't show her—his toughness. He had already stared down two men who had formerly been known as "bad." Once they backed down from Elfego Baca, their reputations changed.

Raphael, however, still appeared to be unimpressed.

"They backed down from your reputation," he was saying on this day. "Not from you, and not from your gun."

Elfego Baca looked down at the .32 Colt he'd started wearing on his hip whenever he wasn't wearing a badge. It was his "lawyer" gun, and he was also wearing it in his Tivoli job.

"Not from my gun, huh?"

Raphael touched the .45 he was wearing on his own hip.

"This is a gun," he said.

"Only if you know how to use it," Elfego said.

"I can shoot."

"Anybody can shoot," Elfego said as they walked past a faro table. He paused a moment to watch the dealer. He had a feeling the man was cheating, but he had not yet been able to catch him at it.

"It's hitting what you shoot at that's important."

"I can hit what I shoot at," Raphael said, though without much conviction.

"Every time?"

The younger man snorted.

"No one can hit what they shoot at every time."

"My brother could," Elfego said, "and so can I."

"Can't be done."

"Certainly not by Numero Ocho."

Raphel stopped walking. Elfego took two more steps, then stopped and turned around.

"Why do you take every chance to say something bad about him?" Raphael asked.

"Because he is a gangster," Elfego said, "and a coward."

"He's not a coward!"

Elfego just shrugged. He needled Raphael about Numero Ocho for two reasons. Partially just to get the boy's goat about his hero, but also because he still thought that Raphael took everything he said back to the gang leader.

"If you're so brave," Raphael went on, "why haven't you faced him yet?"

"He hasn't come to my side of the International Bridge yet."

"Why don't you go over there?" Raphael asked. "Are you afraid?"

"Cautious."

Raphael laughed derisively and said, "That is the same as afraid."

"If you think that," Elfego said, "you have a lot to learn if you want to live to be twenty."

"I am twenty."

"Of course you are."

The conversation ended when Elfego positioned Raphael by the front door and told him to watch for trouble. Then he grabbed one of his other men and told him to watch Raphael.

"Watch him . . . for what?" the man asked. He was an ex-policeman, American rather than Mexican, one of the men Elfego had hired himself, so that he had no allegiance to anyone but Elfego. "Do you think he's . . . stealing?"

"No," Elfego said, "I just think he may not be very careful about who he lets in."

The man shrugged and said, "Okay, boss."

Elfego was wondering how many times—if any—Numero Ocho might have sent men into the Tivoli to take a look at him. It struck him that he was not the only one being cautious.

On the other hand, it was not like Elfego Baca to be cautious. His philosophy had always been to face trouble head-on, and sometimes—as with the *jacal*—to just go out and attack it. Perhaps, in his old age, he was erring on the side of caution when it came to Numero Ocho. Instead of waiting for the man to make the first move, why not just go out and instigate something and get it over with?

For about ten days after that Elfego made sure that Numero Ocho knew where he'd be all the time. He also made sure that his wife was not with him during that time. He was not sure if her presence would have any effect on the gang leader, but he knew it would on him. He'd probably be so concerned for her that he'd end up getting himself killed.

When he told her for the fifth time in ten days that they could not go out for dinner, she finally asked, "What are you up to?"

"What do you mean?" he asked. "I'm not up to anything."

"Yes, you are," she said. "You don't want to be seen in public with me."

"That is silly."

"It means one of two things."

"What two things?"

"Either you have a fancy woman that you're seeing," she said, "or you're planning something dangerous."

He paused in his preparation to leave for work.

"And wouldn't my having a fancy woman somewhere," he asked, "be the same as doing something dangerous?"

"Elfego Baca," she said, "if you go out and get yourself killed after surviving all these years—"

He took her by the shoulders and said, "*Querida,* I am not going to get killed, I am just going to finish something I have ignored for too long."

"Well, then," she said, "finish it and take me to supper."

"Yes, ma'am," he said. "I will finish it today."

Chapter Fifty-two

When he got to the Tivoli, Elfego pulled Raphael from his position and told one of the other men to replace him.

"Where are we going?" Raphael asked as he followed Elfego out of the place.

"I'm going to teach you two things today," Elfego said. "If you don't learn a thing from either one, I'm going to fire you."

"Fire me? Why? I do my job."

"Yes, you do," Elfego said, "but for which employer?"

"Huh?"

"Never mind," Elfego said. "I'll explain later."

"Where are we going now?" The boy was surprised that he had to run to keep up with the man with the stubbier legs.

"We're going to the livery stable."

"What for?"

"We're going to take a ride."

"But . . . I don't own a horse."

"I'll rent you one!"

During the times that Elfego had one of the other men watch Raphael it was reported that, on occasion, something was handed to the young man by a man who entered. Elfego took this to mean that Raphael was accepting his pay from Numero Ocho while, at the same time, allowing the gang leader's men to enter the Tivoli. The men had been instructed to turn away anyone they deemed "undesirable," and if there was any problem with that to send for him. In the five weeks he had been working there, Raphael had never sent for Elfego. Most of the other men who had duty at the front doors had, at least once.

This could have meant that Raphael was very good at his job, but Elfego chose to believe that the young man did not know an undesirable when he saw one.

Elfego Baca was going to show him one today.

They picked up two horses at the livery, Elfego's and a rental for Raphael. Elfego took the boy just to the outskirts of town, to a clearing, where they dismounted.

"What are we doing here?" Raphael asked.

"I want to see you shoot."

"At what?" Raphael looked around. He saw the shattered remains of many bottles, and a lot of cans lying around.

"I come out here and shoot once in a while," Elfego said. In fact, he came out here occasionally with some of the other men, the older ones who used to be policemen or detectives. It was a way to keep their eyes sharp, as there was very little shooting—thank the saints—during the course of their jobs at the Tivoli.

Elfego walked over to a barrel that was set up against a tree. All of the men he shot with came here whenever they could and deposited fresh cans and bottles in the barrel, so that they'd all have something to shoot at whenever they felt the need.

Elfego took out five cans and five bottles and very carefully set them on a log, then he walked back to where Raphael was standing. He counted off sixty paces.

"Shoot," Elfego said.

"At what?"

"You choose," the older man said. "Can or bottle."

Raphael frowned, then drew his gun, sighted, and fired. A can jumped off the log and rolled onto the ground.

"Ha!" Raphael shouted. "Got it."

"You got a can," Elfego said.

"So? You said to shoot anything."

"You were aiming at a bottle."

Raphael looked shocked that Elfego would know that. He had, indeed, been aiming at a bottle, and had been shocked when he hit one of the cans.

"I was not!" he lied.

"All right, then," Elfego said. "Now you will shoot at what I tell you. Hit the second bottle from the right."

"The . . . right?" Raphael asked.

"The second from the end of the log," Elfego said. He was not here to teach the boy his left from his right. Right from *wrong* was much more important than right from left.

"Second . . ." Raphael said. He sighted and pulled the trigger, striking the log just below the third bottle.

"You're low and pulling left," Elfego said.

The boy tried again, struck the ground in front of the log.

"Try again."

This time when he fired he struck the bottle.

"I hit it!"

"It took you three tries."

"They're too far."

"They are not."

"Then you hit one."

"All right," Elfego said. "You pick."

"That last can, at the other end of the lo—"

Elfego drew and fired in one motion. The can leaped into the air before falling to the ground and rolling.

"You . . . you didn't even aim," Raphael said.

"You don't have to," Elfego said. "You don't aim a gun, you point it."

"Huh? You were lucky."

"Pick another."

This time the boy picked a bottle. Elfego drew and shattered it, then holstered the gun.

"I don't miss," Elfego said.

"Everybody misses," Raphael said.

"I don't."

"Impossible."

"Do you want to bet?"

Raphael narrowed his eyes suspiciously.

"What kind of bet?"

"If I miss even once, I'll give you a raise."

"You only have to miss once?"

"That's right."

"Out of how many shots?"

"You pick."

"A dozen," the boy said right away, "not counting the two you already hit."

"Agreed."

Elfego took out his gun and reloaded the spent cartridges, then returned it to his holster. He wished he'd brought his other gun, as well. He could have fired with both hands and won the bet sooner.

"Wait," Raphael said. "What if I lose the bet?"

"That's easy," Elfego said. He folded his arms across his chest. On both hands he was wearing tight leather gloves. "If I hit twelve in a row without a miss, you have to take me to Numero Ocho."

Raphael swallowed.

"W-what makes you think I could do that?"

"You work for him."

"I—I work for you."

"And for him," Elfego said. "I am not a fool, boy. Don't treat me like one."

"But—"

"You're reporting back to him," Elfego said. "You're a spy for him."

"H-how long have you known?"

"I suspected from the very beginning," Elfego said. "I've known for a few weeks."

"B-but how?"

"You've been seen taking payments from his men."

"But . . . why did you suspect me?"

"You don't hide your admiration for him."

"That's all?"

Elfego shrugged.

"I knew it was not any of the other men. It might have been one of the ones I fired, but I was fairly certain it was you."

"Then why keep me working for you?"

"So I could watch you," Elfego said. "So I could send some messages to Numero Ocho. But also so I could save you."

"Save me?" the boy asked. "From what?"

"From yourself, mostly," Elfego said. "You're

on the wrong track, boy. I'm going to put you on the right one."

"Why?" Raphael asked. "Why would you want to do that?"

"Because," Elfego Baca said, "nobody did it for me when I was your age."

"You?" Raphael asked. "When you were my age you were already a hero."

"Because I had done something very foolish," Elfego said. "If someone had set me straight before that, I believe my life might have been much different. Maybe not better, but different."

"You're Elfego Baca, the hero of the Friscos," Raphael said. "What could be better?"

"A lot of things," Elfego said. To himself he admitted that he could have been arrested and tried fewer times than he was, certainly shot or stabbed fewer times. To the boy he simply said, "Lots of things."

"I don't understand. . . ."

"It's simple," Elfego said. "I want to see Numero Ocho today. If you lose the bet, you take me to him."

"He—he'll kill me."

"He won't," Elfego said. "I'm sure he wants to see me almost as badly as I want to see him."

Raphael hesitated.

"Do we have a bet?"

The boy swallowed, then made his decision.

"We have a bet."

Chapter Fifty-three

"I still don't believe it."

They were riding back to town, heading for the livery to return the horses. Elfego intended for them to walk across the International Bridge to go and see Numero Ocho.

"I told you I don't miss," Elfego said.

"I know, but . . ."

Raphael's jaw all but dropped to the floor when he witnessed Elfego Baca's prowess with a gun—and with a .32, at that. Not even a .45, which Raphael had always considered a real man's gun. At least, that was what Numero Ocho had told him.

After setting up ten targets—five bottles, five cans—Elfego had drawn and fired very quickly. He emptied the six shots from his gun a first time.

Five bottles had shattered, and one can had gone flying. He'd reloaded and fired quickly again. The remaining four cans had gone flying, and then he shot the second one two more times, keeping it dancing in the air until he was out of bullets.

Then he'd reloaded under the amazed eye of Raphael.

"Don't ever wait to reload your gun," Elfego instructed him. "Even if you only fire once, replace that spent round with a live one. That may be the round that saves your life." When the boy didn't respond, Elfego holstered his pistol and looked at him. "Do you understand?"

"Yes," Raphael said, "I understand."

"Come on," Elfego had said, "let's head back."

Now they returned their horses to the livery and started back toward the center of town on foot.

"Time for you to pay up," Elfego said.

"Elfego," Raphael said, "I—I cannot—"

Elfego grabbed his arm, stopping their progress.

"You have to pay off your bet, Raphael," Elfego said.

"I—I can tell you where to go," the young man said, "b-but I cannot take you there. He will kill me."

"He won't."

"Will you kill him?"

"No."

"Then—"

"I just want you to see something," Elfego said. "That's why you have to come."

Raphael saw that he had no way out. If he was a man, he had to pay his debt.

"Very well."

He followed Elfego Baca.

Chapter Fifty-four

They stopped first at the Tivoli so Elfego could retrieve his second gun, and then they walked to the bridge.

Raphael took Elfego to several places he thought Numero Ocho might be. In each case it turned out that the man was not there. Late in the afternoon, Elfego got tired of following the boy around.

"Raphael."

The younger man stopped, turned, and faced Elfego. His shoulders were hunched, as if he knew what to expect.

"You've been leading me on a merry chase through Juarez, Raphael," Elfego said. "Did you think I'd change my mind?"

Raphael shrugged and said, "I hoped . . ." but he did not finish.

"Come," Elfego said, "take me to the place Numero Ocho uses as a headquarters."

"But—"

"Don't tell me you don't know," Elfego said. "Just take me there."

Raphael's shoulders slumped, and he said, "As you wish Elfego."

Numero Ocho's headquarters was in a cellar, the entrance of which was in an alley alongside an undistinguished building. Elfego wasn't concerned with what was upstairs, only downstairs.

Being with Raphael gained Elfego entry at the door, already a chink in the so-called armor of the gang leader. If Elfego were there to kill Numero Ocho, the gangster would be dead.

When they reached the cellar Elfego could feel that Raphael had practically stopped breathing. The room was full of men, but Elfego had eyes for only one—or "eight."

"Which one of you is Ocho?" he demanded loudly. "I am Elfego Baca."

The room fell quiet, and one man stood. He was tall, well built, and hard looking, in his thirties. He was in his element among his gang members, but Elfego had messages to send. One to Raphael, one to the other men in the room, and the last one to Numero Ocho himself.

"I am Numero Ocho."

Elfego remembered what Francisquita had said about a man calling himself after a number—and it did sound ridiculous.

He strode purposefully across the room and wiped the arrogant smirk off the gang leader's face—not with a punch but with an open-handed slap. He followed this with a left hook to the stomach before the sound of the slap had faded. He slapped the man twice more, stinging, open-handed, insulting slaps that reddened the man's face and brought blood from his lip.

As with most bullies, faced with a man who had absolutely no fear, the gang leader turned to flee. Elfego helped him along with a vicious kick in the pants.

It had taken only moments, and Elfego quickly turned on the gang and drew both of his guns.

"That was your great leader!" he shouted. "He'll still be running when he hits Mexico City. Who wants to be the new leader? Come on. Step up!"

The men exchanged fearful glances, convinced that they had a madman in their midst.

"Very well," Elfego said. "I have an excellent memory for faces. If I ever see any of you in the Tivoli, I'll kill you. No questions asked, and no warning. Understood?"

There was a murmur from the gang, which Elfego took as a yes.

"Raphael works for me," Elfego said. "Any

man who touches him will have to deal with me. Do you understand that? Do you?"

This time the answer came louder, satisfying Elfego that they understood.

"Raphael!" he said, and backed toward the door with his guns still out. Raphael made his decision quickly, drew his gun, and covered Elfego's exit.

Outside they holstered their guns, and Elfego said, "Let's go, quickly, before they get brave."

They made their way to the bridge and crossed back into El Paso.

Raphael was quiet all the way back to the Tivoli. When they reached it, they stopped outside before entering.

"Elfego, you said back there that I work for you," the younger man said. "Is that true? I am not fired?"

"Did you learn anything today?" Elfego said. "Remember, I said if you don't learn anything then I would fire you."

"*Sí,*" Raphael said, "I learned something very important."

"What did you learn?" Elfego asked.

Raphael squared his shoulders, firmed his jaw, and looked the older man in the eye.

"I learned that you are truly still Elfego Baca!"

Elfego stared at the boy for a few moments, then said, "Get inside and go to work."

Chapter Fifty-five

The end came very quickly at the Tivoli for Elfego Baca.

One of his men called for him at the front door because a customer was being both belligerent and rude. Allowed to enter, the young man would certainly have caused a ruckus.

Elfego refused him entry.

"This is unacceptable," the young man said. "Do you know who I am?"

"I don't care if you're the King of France," Elfego said. "You are not coming in."

Enraged, the young man had the audacity to swing at Elfego, who deftly avoided the blow and delivered one of his own. It was little more than a tap, but delivered to the young man's belly it knocked the wind out of him.

Elfego arrested him and had him thrown into a cell. When it was later discovered that the young man was the son of the chief of police of Juarez, Elfego knew he was finished at the Tivoli.

He gathered his bosses, Rebia, Revilla, Asteca, and Lopez in their office, and bid them *adiós!* He knew it would be a hardship for them to try to keep him on after the incident. Besides, he had the security of the Tivoli running like clockwork, and he had rid them of Numero Ocho's interference.

It was time for Elfego Baca to move on—again.

Once again Elfego's friend, Senator Albert Bacon Fall, came to his aid after he left the Tivoli. The senator arranged for the Department of the Interior to appoint Elfego Indian agent for southeastern Utah. This was perhaps the farthest Elfego had ventured from his beloved New Mexico, and in taking the job he left his wife behind in Socorro.

Although he knew very little about Indians, Elfego thought he could do the job simply by applying the same virtues he always applied to his various endeavors—logic, intelligence, and courage.

Others might have listed his various virtues differently—bullheadedness, impetuousness, and . . . well, courage.

Chapter Fifty-six

Being the Indian agent for Southeast Utah basically meant mediating disputes between the settlers and the Paiute Indians. Elfego didn't know much about Indians, but he knew a lot about people, and as far as he was concerned, Indians were people.

"I'm tellin' you, Baca," Henry Davis said, "there's gonna be a war."

Elfego stared at the five cards in his hand. He would have enjoyed the hand more without Davis chattering in his ear about Indians, though. Only a week on the job, but so far he'd managed to avoid contact with them.

"Are you listenin', Baca?" the man asked.

"Every word, Mr. Davis," Elfego said. "I raise."

"You raise?" one of the other players asked.

"That's right."

"But . . . you checked."

Elfego looked across the table at the man.

"Are you saying I can't check and raise?"

The man looked at the other two players in the game, who both looked away. Then he looked at Elfego, and the gun on the table next to his chips. Elfego never played poker without having his .32 on the table. It was a practice he had started just a few years ago. Because he had grown heavier, and older, men often took this to mean he'd grown softer. Having his gun on the table usually dispelled that thought.

"Uh, no," the man said, "go ahead, raise."

"*Gracias,*" Elfego said, "I raise."

Two of the other players called. The man who had argued briefly dropped out. Elfego took the hand with three kings.

"Baca! I need help here," Davis said, "and all you can do is play cards?"

"All right, Davis," Elfego said, dragging in his chips. "What's the problem?"

"I told you," Davis said. "I got a band of murderin' Paiutes comin' to my place tomorrow mornin'."

"For what?"

"They want my women!"

"What women do you have there?"

"My wife and my daughter. They're scared ta death!"

293

That caught Elfego's attention.

"Deal me out, boys," he said, and turned his attention fully to Davis. The other players ignored the game and listened as well.

"Davis, the Paiutes are not murderers."

"They're Indians, ain't they?" one of the poker players said. "Don't that make 'em murderers?"

Elfego gave the man a hard stare.

"Mr. Davis," Elfego said, "you tell your wife and your daughter not to worry. I will be at your place early tomorrow morning."

"Good," Davis said with relief. "Will you be bringing a posse?"

"I am not a lawman, Mr. Davis," Elfego said. "I don't have the authority to form a posse. But don't worry, I will take care of everything."

"But—"

"Please," Elfego said. "Go home and stay with your women until I arrive tomorrow."

"Well . . . okay," Davis said. At least the Indian agent was listening and was going to do something.

As Davis left, Elfego was looking off into the distance, missing New Mexico and his wife.

"Mr. Baca?" one of the players asked.

"Hmm? Yes?"

"Are you, uh, still playin'?"

Elfego looked at the table, then at the men around it. He came out of his reveries and started collecting his chips to cash out.

"No," Elfego said, "I am sorry, gentlemen, but

I'm through for the evening. Thank you."

The last thing he did was take his gun off the table and holster it, and then walk away. Collectively, the other men at the table breathed a sigh of relief.

Elfego cashed in his winnings and went to his office. He felt as out of place there as he had when he first arrived. The town of Longview, Utah, was not to his liking. It was very unlike the towns where he had spent most of his past.

The way of life here was very different also, and he did not think he would be able to get used to it. He realized that by accepting this job he had not been fair to the people who lived here, to the U.S. government, to his friend Albert Fall, who had gotten him the job, to his wife, and, most of all, to himself.

He decided that he would deal with the Indians that were bothering the Davis family tomorrow, and then he would wire his resignation to Washington and return to Socorro, where he belonged.

Chapter Fifty-seven

The next morning, Henry Davis's wife and sixteen-year-old daughter greeted Elfego Baca as if he were the second coming. They insisted on giving him coffee and making him breakfast, and he had no choice but to accept. Their gratitude embarrassed him, especially since he didn't really know if he was going to be able to help them. Elfego had spent more of his life fighting white men than Indians.

"Here they come," Henry Davis said from the window.

"How many of them?" his wife asked.

"Six."

"Oh, Daddy," the daughter said.

"Now, take it easy, Esther," her mother said.

"We have Mr. Baca here to protect us, remember."

Elfego got up from the table and walked to the window. He saw six Indian braves riding toward the house. He checked both his guns, tucked them away, and turned to Henry Davis.

"Don't come out unless I call you, understand?"

Davis nodded and said, "I can cover you from here with my rifle."

"No," Elfego said, "I don't want them to see a rifle barrel sticking out a window. Just sit tight and wait for me."

"God be with you," Mrs. Davis said.

"I hope so, ma'am," Elfego said, and stepped outside.

When the six braves saw him they halted their progress. Elfego started walking out toward them. He wondered why they were picking on Henry Davis, who had a very small spread. Granted, his wife and daughter were pretty, both with yellow hair that would certainly look unusual to an Indian. There must have been more to it than that, though.

Elfego walked to within hailing distance of the Indians. He had expected to see war paint, but there was none. In truth, these six looked rather meek.

"I am called Elfego Baca," he said. "I am the Indian agent here."

"Baca," one of them said. "We have heard of you."

"Really?" Elfego was surprised that his fame had spread this far, to the ears of a band of Indians in Utah.

"We were told of your coming," the first Indian said. "We were told that you were coming to help us."

"I'm here to help you and the white man get along," Elfego said. Apparently, they'd heard his name but not his reputation. He felt slightly foolish for a moment for thinking that these Indians might have heard of him.

"Why are you here?" Elfego asked.

"We come to talk to the white man who lives here," the Indian said. "He is called Davis."

"What are you called?" Elfego asked the spokesman.

"Running Hawk."

"What do you want here, Running Hawk?"

"To talk to Davis."

"Mr. Davis seems to think you're here for his women," Elfego said. "We can't allow that kind of thing around here, you know."

Running Hawk turned and spoke to the other five braves in their own language, and they all began to laugh.

"What is so funny?" Elfego asked.

"Why would we want Davis's women?" Running Hawk asked. "We have our own squaws. They cook for us, they chew the leather to make our clothes soft. Why would we want white women?"

Elfego was confused.

"You didn't tell Davis you wanted his women?"

"We came," Running Hawk said, "and Davis would not talk. He said to come back today. We are back, to talk to Davis."

"About what?"

"Meat."

"Meat?"

"Davis has cows," Running Hawk said. "We want some."

"So you don't want to steal his women," Elfego said, "you want to steal his cows."

"We are not here to steal," Running Hawk said, and he seemed genuinely insulted. "We are here to trade."

"You want to trade with Davis for his cows?"

"Yes," Running Hawk said.

"How many?"

"Enough for meat to feed our families," Running Hawk said. "Maybe . . . five cows each month."

"And you have things to trade?"

"We do." Running Hawk waved, and another brave rode forward, leading a packhorse.

"Wait," Elfego said, "I don't need to see your items for trade. Wait here and I will get Davis."

"We will wait."

Elfego walked back to the house and called for Davis to come out. As the door opened and the man started out, Elfego saw that he was holding his rifle.

"Leave that rifle inside!" he snapped.

Davis obeyed and came out timidly.

"Did you talk to these braves?" Elfego asked. "Did you ask them what they wanted before you assumed they wanted your women?"

"Well . . . no . . ."

"Why not?"

"Well . . . they're Indians . . . savages. . . . What else could they want from us?"

"Food," Elfego said. "They want to trade with you each month for meat."

"Meat?"

Elfego nodded.

"They don't want my women?"

"They have their own women, and they're very happy with them," Elfego said.

"And . . . you believe them?"

"I know when a man is insulted, Mr. Davis," Elfego said. "Their spokesman is named Running Hawk, and when I suggested that he wanted to steal your women—or your cattle—he was real insulted. Yeah, I believe them."

"Well . . . I'll be . . ."

"Next time," Elfego said, "don't be so quick to jump the gun, Davis. Now come on, I'll introduce you to Running Hawk, and the two of you can dicker."

"Well, I'll be . . ." Davis said, scratching his head.

Elfego walked Davis out to where Running Hawk was waiting, thinking how stupid Americans were. He was definitely going back to New Mexico, where he belonged.

Interlude

"And so I have spent most of my days since then in New Mexico, in Socorro, and in Albuquerque, where I presently reside."

"And have you stayed out of trouble all this time?" the reporter asked.

"Well . . . hardly . . . I continue to appear in court, very often to defend men charged with drunk and disorderly."

"Why such . . . pedestrian cases?" the reporter asked. "Why not something along the lines of, oh . . . General Salazar?"

Elfego laughed.

"Those cases are few and far between, my young friend. Most of the cases I take into court are boring. Sometimes, I have to make my own excitement."

"Such as?"

"I will tell you something off the record."

The reporter looked down at the pages of his notebook he had filled, and thought that he had enough material to grant Elfego Baca this request.

"All right."

"Some years back I was forced into bankruptcy. I made some bad investments. My debtors had a habit of coming to my office to demand their money."

"And you didn't let them in?"

"Oh, I let them in," Elfego said, "and I left my gun out on my desk in plain sight. As irate as they were when they entered the room, they left just as meekly."

The reporter laughed at the idea of Elfego Baca's gun—not even in his hand or on his person—scaring his debtors away.

"Once I had to make an insurance claim on a building I owned that burned down. I made the claim for twelve hundred dollars."

"Did they pay?'

"They offered me six."

"What did you do?"

"I went up to their office wearing my guns," Elfego said, "and I got my twelve hundred."

"I think I see why you say you have made your own excitement over the past few years," the reporter said.

"Well, it was not always of my making. Several

years ago, a friend of mine was being taken into custody by a policeman who was being unnecessarily rough. I stepped in to make a complaint, and the policeman tried to get rough with me."

"You didn't shoot him!" the reporter said, aghast.

"No, no," Elfego said. "I am occasionally foolhardy, my friend, but rarely downright stupid."

"So what did you do?"

"At the time I had taken to carrying a pocket watch of the potato variety. Do you know it?"

"Indeed, I do," the reporter said. "A rather large, cumbersome thing, as I remember."

"Very large," Elfego said, "so large as to be able to be used as a . . . weapon, in some instances."

"You didn't."

"I did," Elfego said. "I hit the officer with it."

"And you were arrested."

"Oh, yes," Elfego said. "I was taken before a judge, who scolded me, charged me with drunk and disorderly, and sentenced me to thirty days in jail."

"And did you serve all thirty days?"

"Why not?" Elfego asked. "Room and board and three square meals. It was an excellent rest for me—and a profitable one."

"Profitable? How so?"

"Well, you see, the jail is in Old Albuquerque, and the night court where I was sentenced is in New Albuquerque."

"So?"

"Prisoners are given seventy-five cents a day for food while serving their sentence," Elfego Baca said, "and the jailer is given seventy-five cents for each prisoner in his jail."

"So you made seventy-five cents a day while you were there?"

Elfego Baca smiled.

"A dollar fifty."

"How so?"

"Because the judge rarely ventured into Old Albuquerque, he was unaware of the fact that, at that time, I happened to have the job as jailer."

"Amazing!" the reporter said. "You were paid for having yourself in your own jail?"

Elfego laughed aloud at the memory. "And I made twenty-two dollars and fifty cents in the process."

Both men laughed together now, and as the laughter faded so, too, did Elfego Baca's energy.

"I think I have told you all that I can, young man," Elfego said. "It's time for me to turn in, and tomorrow to return to Albuquerque."

"Mr. Baca," the reporter said, "I have only one more question to ask."

Elfego stood, rubbed his ass, which had fallen asleep while sitting for so long, and said, "Ask it."

"All these stories that you have told me," the reporter said. "Are they all . . . totally true?"

"Totally true?" Elfego said after a moment of

thought. "When is anything totally true? Everything is . . . embellished in the telling and the retelling, is it not?"

"I suppose," the younger man said.

"I will tell you this . . . they are as true as any story you will ever hear about me . . . as true as any story I will ever tell."

"But—"

"Good night, young man," Elfego Baca said, "and please, make sure you send me a copy of the story. I'll want to see what embellishments you might make on them yourself."

Epilogue

Elfego Baca ran for public office several more times after 1940, after the "door" ceremony and after the tribute article came out in *The Albuquerque Tribune*. In each instance, he was defeated.

In 1943 he tried to open yet another business, an imported-goods store. After he brandished his guns and chased off a couple of government employees who wanted to talk to him about his building being abandoned, that too soon failed.

In 1944, when he was seventy-nine, he moved his residence to a smaller building and ran for the office of district attorney. He campaigned heavily for the office but was again—and for the last time—defeated.

He had one last desire that would not be fulfilled—he would like to have seen his life made into a motion picture.

It did not happen.

On August 27, 1945, Elfego Baca finished his dinner and looked across at his wife of nearly sixty years. They'd had some problems over the years, mostly due to his foolishness. He had begun to drink heavily during the 1930s, which precipitated fights. Once, in 1932, he tried to have a restraining order taken out against her because she persisted in entering his office without knocking, and he felt a need for privacy. After that she left him, went to live with one of their children in California. She soon returned, though, he moderated his drinking, and their life continued on together.

On this night she began to clear the table, and he said, "I'm going into the parlor to listen to the radio."

"What are you going to listen to?"

"Clinton Anderson is supposed to speak."

"Ah."

Elfego was still interested in politics, and Anderson, the United States Representative from New Mexico, had recently been appointed Secretary of Agriculture by President Truman. Elfego Baca continued to be a staunch supporter of any politician from his beloved New Mexico.

"I will finish cleaning up and join you."

Elfego felt badly that Francisquita had to continue cooking and cleaning up after him. He had always wanted to give her servants to do that, but alas, that was another dream that had not come to pass.

He left the room and went into the parlor to sit by the radio. Francisquita finished cleaning the table and put the dishes in the sink. She decided to go and sit with her husband to listen to Clinton Anderson speak, then return to do the dishes.

As she entered the parlor she heard the radio droning on and saw her husband sitting in an easy chair next to it. His head was back, his eyes were closed, and he was not breathing. He was eighty years old, and he never did get to hear his politician speak.

And so ended an era . . .

. . . and a legend was born.

Author's Notes

In the telling of this story two books were invaluable as research sources: *The Mexican American* by Kyle S. Crichton, which has also been known by the title *Law and Order, LTD.: The Rousing Life of Elfego Baca of New Mexico*. This book was published by the Santa Fe New Mexico Publishing Corp. in 1928, and was reprinted by Arno Press in 1974. Obviously, the book appeared during Elfego Baca's lifetime, and much of what the author wrote he claimed to have heard from Elfego Baca himself.

The second book is *Incredible Elfego Baca: Good Man, Bad Man of the Old West* by Howard Bryan, with a foreword by Rudolpho Anaya. This book, published in 1993 by the Clear Light Press, took Elfego Baca's life right through to his death in 1945. In this book Bryan sometimes contradicts the Crichton book. Because of this, I took the liberty of combining material from both books in order to tell my story.

The facts are these: There *was* an incident where Elfego Baca held of approximately eighty cowboys while holed up in a building called a *jacal,* when he was nineteen. He *did* go on to have a colorful life, to hold several public offices, to be a *bastonero,* a private detective, a deputy sheriff, a sheriff, and a lawyer. He *did* meet someone named William Bonney, although it's debatable as to whether or not this was the Billy the Kid who was later involved in the Lincoln County War. He *did* meet Pancho Villa; *did* defend General Salazar; *did* work in the Tivoli in Albuquerque, where he met Mary Garden; and *did* slap the taste out of the mouth of a gangster named Numero Ocho.

Elfego Baca was survived by his wife, his son, his five daughters, eight grandchildren, and two great-grandchildren.

The rest is either a figment of my imagination or the way I'd like to think his life might have gone.

Legend

LOREN D. ESTLEMAN, ELMER KELTON, JUDY ALTER, JAMES REASONER, JANE CANDIA COLEMAN, ED GORMAN, ROBERT J. RANDISI

For the first time, these amazing talents—combined winners of 14 Spur Awards!—have joined forces, and the result is truly the stuff of legend. Together they recount the life of Lyle Speaks, from his hardscrabble boyhood in Texas to his later years as an aging cattle rancher in Montana, years in which his colorful past may yet come back to haunt him. From one end of the West to the other, Lyle's exploits made him famous—admired by some, feared by others. But now Lyle wants to set the record straight. No matter what the cost.

___4496-X $5.99 US/$6.99 CAN

THE GHOST WITH BLUE EYES

ROBERT J. RANDISI

A beautiful little girl with startling blue eyes. Eyes that look up at Lancaster as he fires the shot that kills her. He didn't mean to do it. Why did she have to get in the way just as he drew down on the man he was hired to kill? He asks himself that question every day, but he never finds the answer, or a way to forgive himself. Even before the girl's body is cold, Lancaster hangs up his guns and picks up a bottle. But even the booze can't get those blue eyes out of his head. And when he finds another little girl who needs his help, he knows he's finally found a way to regain his soul . . . even if it costs him his life in the bargain.

___4571-0 $4.50 US/$5.50 CAN

MOVING ON
JANE CANDIA
COLEMAN

Jane Candia Coleman is a magical storyteller who spins brilliant tales of human survival, hope, and courage on the American frontier, and nowhere is her marvelous talent more in evidence than in this acclaimed collection of her finest work. From a haunting story of the night Billy the Kid died, to a dramatic account of a breathtaking horse race, including two stories that won the prestigious Spur Award, here is a collection that reveals the passion and fortitude of its characters, and also the power of a wonderful writer.

___4545-1 $4.99 US/$5.99 CAN

Dorchester Publishing Co., Inc.
P.O. Box 6640
Wayne, PA 19087-8640

Please add $1.75 for shipping and handling for the first book and $.50 for each book thereafter. NY, NYC, and PA residents, please add appropriate sales tax. No cash, stamps, or C.O.D.s. All orders shipped within 6 weeks via postal service book rate. Canadian orders require $2.00 extra postage and must be paid in U.S. dollars through a U.S. banking facility.

Name_____
Address_____
City_____State_____Zip_____
I have enclosed $_____ in payment for the checked book(s).
Payment <u>must</u> accompany all orders. ☐ Please send a free catalog.
      CHECK OUT OUR WEBSITE! www.dorchesterpub.com

GRAVES' RETREAT
ED GORMAN

Cedar Rapids in 1884 is a place where Les Graves has a chance to finally earn the respectability he has always wanted and to marry the woman he loves. Then his brother T. Z. comes into town, bringing with him trouble with a capital T. It seems that T. Z. and his friend Neely have big plans for the local bank where Graves happens to work. And they are counting on Graves' help to pull off the heist. All Graves gets in return for his loyalty is a hard cot in a drafty cell—until a rivalry between two local sheriffs gives him one shot at freedom. But before Graves can return to his peaceful life and the pursuit of the woman of his dreams, there are a few more twists in the trail. . . with trouble around each bend.

___4655-5 $3.99 US/$4.99 CAN

Dorchester Publishing Co., Inc.
P.O. Box 6640
Wayne, PA 19087-8640

Please add $1.75 for shipping and handling for the first book and $.50 for each book thereafter. NY, NYC, and PA residents, please add appropriate sales tax. No cash, stamps, or C.O.D.s. All orders shipped within 6 weeks via postal service book rate. Canadian orders require $2.00 extra postage and must be paid in U.S. dollars through a U.S. banking facility.

Name_____
Address_____
City_____ State_____ Zip_____
I have enclosed $_____ in payment for the checked book(s).
Payment <u>must</u> accompany all orders. ❑ Please send a free catalog.
CHECK OUT OUR WEBSITE! www.dorchesterpub.com

TROUBLE MAN

ED GORMAN

Ray Coyle used to be a gunfighter. And when he gets word his boy has been killed in a gunfight in Coopersville, he has to go there—to bring the body home. But when the old gunfighter steps off the train, he brings his gun with him, along with something else . . . trouble.

___4440-4 $4.99 US/$5.99 CAN

Dorchester Publishing Co., Inc.
P.O. Box 6640
Wayne, PA 19087-8640

Please add $1.75 for shipping and handling for the first book and $.50 for each book thereafter. NY, NYC, and PA residents, please add appropriate sales tax. No cash, stamps, or C.O.D.s. All orders shipped within 6 weeks via postal service book rate. Canadian orders require $2.00 extra postage and must be paid in U.S. dollars through a U.S. banking facility.

Name_____
Address_____
City_____ State_____ Zip_____
I have enclosed $_____ in payment for the checked book(s).
Payment <u>must</u> accompany all orders. ❑ Please send a free catalog.
      CHECK OUT OUR WEBSITE! www.dorchesterpub.com

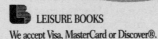